A SPARK OF ADVE~~NTURE~~

JOHN MAYNARD KEYNES AND THE DEGAS AUCTION

BY

DAVID SHIRES

ISBN: 9798756087840

John Maynard Keynes at Charleston by Duncan Grant, 1917

3

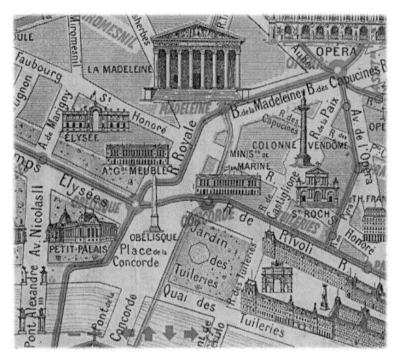

The Robelin Map – Central Paris in 1918

Την πατρίδα μου δεν θα την αφησω με μειωμένη κληρονομιά αλλα με μεγαλύτερη και καλύτερη απο οτι την έλαβα

'My native land I will not leave a diminished heritage but greater and better than when I received it.'

Part of the Ephebic oath sworn by the people of ancient Athens on becoming citizens

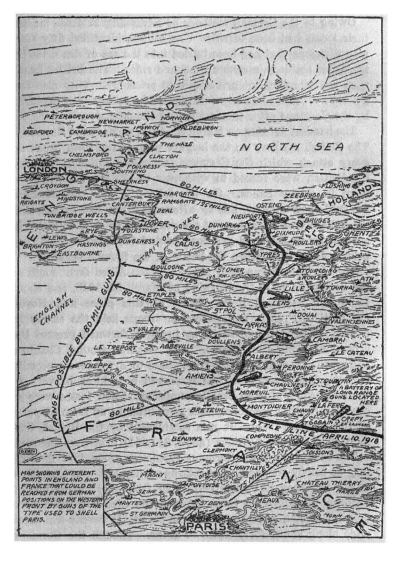

Map showing the range of the 'Supergun' used to shell Paris in 1918

From Project Gutenberg, *The Story of the Great War, Vol. VII*

1

Fitzroy Square

On the Ides of March, 1918, in the fourth year of what is already named The Great War, a taxi trundles past the British Museum's soot-blackened façades into the district of Bloomsbury. In the back of the unheated Hackney Carriage, Maynard, as he is called by those close to him, feels as if the cold has got into his very bones, a malaise brought on by fatigue he thinks, exhaustion actually. He hugs himself for warmth and sinks deeper into the satin-lined Chinchilla overcoat in which he is enveloped.

His mind aches from the past week's trials at the Treasury – the hours of anxiety spent managing an Exchequer engaged in ruinous war-making. He knows the world's economists are the trustees not of civilisation but of its possibilities and so he plans too for the peace that must surely follow. It is his endeavour that this will be the war to end all wars, that poets shall never again write of eyes tearful with sad goodbyes, of angry guns and the slow drawing-down of blinds at dusk. But he fears his dreams of lasting peace are more in hope than expectation. Men, it seems, are stupid.

He steps out of the cab, gives the driver an overly generous tip and walks up to the front door of 33 Fitzroy Square. He'd already noted the make and model of the taxi; a twenty-five horse power, French-made *Panhard & Levassor*, and now congratulates himself on recalling its significance. As Britain has few indigenous motorised cabs of its own, they must be imported. Just three months ago, as the Government's *Head of External Finance*, he had personally signed-off their import licence and added the tax due to the four-hundred million pounds in war loans already channelled through to the French government. Not that they would ever get any of it back. But he blocks the futility of this thought by deploying an excited anticipation of the weekend ahead in heavenly Sussex. He'd be two whole days away from London's damp, foul air and there'd be country walks, wine and good conversation and most deliciously of all, forty-eight hours with the cherubic Georg. His mood begins to change, the melancholy he felt in the taxi lifts. For now anyway.

Outside number 33, a few rays of spring sun glint through the Square's still leafless plane trees and catch the hanging-sign above the door. The lurid orange, black and gold of the Greek letter *Omega* are briefly lit up, making it stand out like a piece of rough graffiti. The other side of the hand-painted board is even less seemly – the representation of a sexualised large-leafed Lily, its stamen protruding provocatively next to a coquettish daisy. Both flowers languish lazily in a glass goblet. What the neighbours must think of one of their more palatial Robert Adam-designed town houses being renamed *Omega Workshops*, given commercial advertisement and frequented by oddly attired artists and their quixotic clientele, takes his mind off his Civil Service tribulations and makes him chuckle. He is still smiling as he puts down his briefcase and brown leather weekend bag, lifts the knocker and gives the grand front door a purposeful bang.

It is opened not by a dutiful servant or uniformed porter but by a wild-eyed boy in his early twenties wearing a wide-brimmed felt hat. He clutches a portfolio of what Maynard takes to be drawings. The young man glances quickly at him and seeing that he is neither vagabond nor artist, dismissively walks away leaving the door open for the visitor to enter. Although he is only thirty-five, Maynard has the appearance and demeanour of a middle-aged man. He wears a white shirt and Cambridge tie and heavy brogues. He looks neat, tidy and staid and of no possible interest to creative types.

"Come in, come in…I suppose you know what you're doing here. I don't," the boy says, vanishing from view into the *Omega's* exhibition gallery. "I'm meant to be meeting Mr Roger Fry but they tell me now he's not here. It really is too bad."

The doorway to the main ground floor reception room has been enlarged into a twelve-foot wide opening and as Maynard rounds its corner, he can see the lad agitatedly pacing up and down amongst the *Avant Garde* displays. *Omega's* designers and artists use pagan colour to decorate the sitting rooms and bedrooms of an intellectual, upper-middle class. There are geometric hand-dyed cushion covers, lampshades, plates, wall coverings and curtains printed with motifs inspired by the dancing human forms of Matisse, Derain and the other *Fauves*. At *Omega*, the old lines between Fine and

9

Decorative art have all but disappeared. These artists are free-thinking experimenters, unbound by the etiquettes or morals of polite society. Here, one may cross boundaries. Anything is possible. Everything is permissible as long as it is beautiful.

Maynard is walking towards the visitor to console him when Duncan bounds down the stairs, suited in loose-fitting corduroy and armed with his customary cane. He has spots of white paint on his hands and eyelashes and across the toes of his unpolished shoes.

"When I heard that determined knock on the door, I knew it was you," he says with a broad smile. "Even in the middle of a war, always punctual, sober and raring to go!"

Maynard's heart skips a beat as the sight of his mop-haired old friend sends a surge of joy through his tired body. In contrast to dull, doughy Englishmen, Duncan's face has a fine-featured nobility. He is an exotic from a colonial background and it is his sensibilities which have guided Maynard through the world of the aesthete.

"My dear chap - has it been another awful week?" continues Duncan as he puts his hands on his friend's shoulders and leans forward to kiss his cheek.

"I think this young man was hoping to see Roger?" Maynard says, gently easing Duncan away.

"He's left for the day. Sorry," says Duncan, turning to look at the boy. He hadn't noticed him and deals out a look of irritation. *Omega* is part of his world and if he wants to kiss his old friend, he will. Here, he can behave as he pleases.

"Yes, a crop-headed woman told me so. She didn't say why Mr Fry had left without letting me know, only that he'd gone. Then she too abandoned me. She was most rude."

"Carrington…" says Duncan conspiratorially as he leans towards Maynard, half-masking his words with the back of his hand. "She's upstairs, drawing…with Gertler." Maynard suppresses his feelings of alarm and continues to smile reassuringly at their visitor.

"She didn't even offer to give Mr Fry a message," says the boy.

Duncan responds but does nothing to smooth things over. "She's not here to answer the door, take messages or to arrange appointments. She's one of our artists," he says.

"Look now," says Maynard stepping forward, exuding placatory charm, "I'm sure Roger will see you very soon. I shall speak to him on Monday and will broker a new arrangement."

"I'm most grateful. My name is Leo Tasken. Please remind him it's about my woodcut prints. I believe they would be most suitable for framing and selling here, the style is influenced by Dufy's *La Dance* and…"

"Yes, and I am sure they are very wonderful. Take this and telephone me on Tuesday. I'll have some news by then," Maynard says, handing over one of his personal calling cards. He takes the boy's arm and gently moves him towards the front door, continuing to smile as he leads him outside. As the lad makes to say his goodbyes, the light of the late afternoon sky strikes the side of his face and fires-up his dark eyes.

"Can we drop you anywhere? We're about to take a taxi south, if that's of any interest..." says Maynard.

"I'm not going your way."

"Perhaps another time?"

"I think it unlikely," replies Leo, uncomfortably. "But I will telephone you regarding my appointment with Mr Fry."

"I shall arrange something advantageous, be assured."

As Maynard says goodbye and closes the door, he catches one of Duncan's knowing looks but moves the conversation on.

"If Gertler is here, I'd like to be somewhere else please."

"He seems alright. Peace has broken out. And Carrington's been extolling the virtues of country living – how calming it is, how beneficial to the creative spirit."

"They could both certainly do with some sort of balm. For a declared pacifist, Mr Mark Gertler is remarkably prone to violent outbursts. Can he not see the contradiction in that position? I'd rather not have to intervene again."

"Lytton's presence that night was a provocation you must agree?"

Maynard shrugs and puts his hand on Duncan's shoulder.

"Let's leave this talk of difficult people behind us now - an early supper at the Savoy and the weekend at Charleston beckons! Neither of us are living in uneducated poverty nor dying in a Flanders trench so out of respect to those who are, let us go now and celebrate our happy good fortune."

2

Seed Planting at The Savoy

Maynard and Duncan walk to Tottenham Court Road to find a taxi. Heavy clouds and a chill in the air signals the coming of night and cold rain and as the shops darken and close, office workers hurry out onto the pavements to start their Friday night journeys home armed with black umbrellas.

The two friends hail a cab and bid the driver take them south to The Strand. They make chit-chat happily enough, Duncan telling of a new still life painting he's been working on and a sketch made of Bunny smoking a pipe. Maynard tries his best to remain light-hearted and speaks of his plans to redecorate his rooms at Gordon Square but it isn't long before his Whitehall frustrations spill over. Duncan knows his friend's days there can be fraught, spent as they are managing the flow of money and supplies between Britain and its allies and that at times it greatly wears him down. He is sympathetic but he also thinks it self-inflicted. Maynard should never have agreed to work for the war mongers of Government in the first place, it had been against his own good counsel.

Maynard snarls out a string of complaints and says that he feels like Wellington during his battles against Napoleon – that he is involved in two wars; one against a foreign adversary, the other against the obstructive contingents on his own side – a plodding, protocol-bound Civil Service and the damnable politicians of Westminster and their City banker accomplices. Even after sitting down at their restaurant table, he rails against his situation throughout the *salade de homard* and *pate de fois gras* set before them. In the high-ceilinged dining room, amongst gilt-edged mirrors and potted palms, such is the wartime rationing at The Savoy Grill.

"...they go out of their way to make my life hell – some of the dolts still hate me for showing them up during the *Specie Payments* fiasco. I saved them from a debacle of their own making but as ever, the talentless don't like to be confronted with their own ineptitude."

"Who does?!"

Duncan is trying his best to lighten the mood but is failing badly.

"That Bank of England bastard Cunliffe even tried to have me dismissed."

"So there are others who can't forgive you?" says Duncan, with a knowing look. Maynard frowns back.

"Cannot our friends see that it's possible to be both pacifist and protagonist in bringing this damnable war to the swiftest conclusion?" he replies.

"And can you not see the contradiction in that position?" Duncan says with a mischievous smile, throwing Maynard's own words back at him. "Look, I understand why you're doing it but they don't."

"Bunny, Jinny and Lytton now won't speak to me. The rest won't even speak about me," says Maynard.

"I have tried explaining your arguments to them but…"

"You mustn't become my apologist, they'll end up hating you too."

Maynard throws down his cutlery in distressed exasperation. "They know what I'm doing is for the greater good surely?" he says. "I'm an outsider with insider skills so why not use them. One can improve things, make a better world."

"Our friends think your insider chums will never allow that to happen."

"Chumps, you mean. Most bankers and MPs are idiots – duffers who are only there by the good fortune of family connections and attending the right school."

Duncan opens his mouth to change the subject but is stopped in his tracks.

"Ill-gotten gains from the captive markets of the British Empire have camouflaged their incompetence for years - all they had to do was count the money," Maynard continues. He is in full-flow now and won't be stopped. "Well, that's changing. The world is at war and won't be the same when it's over. We will have to invest in our people as if they are Current

Assets, the stock in trade of Great Britain Limited. The fools I work with will see this eventually I suppose but meanwhile, I must spend my days spelling things out in words of one syllable, persuading and cajoling, as they try to make sense of something I've explained ten times already."

A waiter arrives, removes their plates and brushes down the table cloth strewn with detritus of Maynard's *hors d'oeuvre*. Even his moustache retains pieces of pâté and bread. Another server brings on the fish course, smiles and leaves them to their one-sided debate, now audible to anyone within a three table range. The other diners have already looked askance at Maynard as he'd greedily fallen upon his supper and having overheard what sounded like seditious rantings, they'd given him sidelong glances of suspicion. Most have decided that he is either drunk, mad, or else some sort of anarchist. Whichever it is, they don't like him.

"Lloyd George's latest brainwave is that if we win the war, he'll raise wages whilst keeping prices low – all so that he's re-elected of course," Maynard goes on. "We'll be witness to the most magnificent peacetime queues the world has ever seen. Lines of people as far as the eye can see for bread, meat, caviar… pianos!"

He takes a pencil from his top pocket, scribbles a faux mathematical formula onto his napkin then turns it round and pushes it across the table towards Duncan with a theatrical flourish.

Length of Queue = Wages ÷ Prices x Supplies

"If Wages constantly increase while Prices and Supplies diminish, then Queue Length tends towards infinity!"

Although no mathematician, Duncan catches his friend's drift and laughs at the comedy of it. But Maynard doesn't smile, instead tossing down his 2B before swigging a mouthful of wine. Duncan looks worried and realises that he needs to act. If things go on like this, the entire weekend will be ruined by Maynard's sullenness.

"Look, here's something to take your mind off it all," he says cheerfully.

The sour look on Maynard's face remains in place as he set about his *filet de sole*. Whatever it is that Duncan is going to show him, he isn't interested. But it's true, Maynard reflects, his involvement with the war Government and the 'ins', the establishment, has meant he'd lost many of his anti-war friends and he grieved on it daily. But he would find a way to make them love him again, he would. Somehow, he must.

With his fine fingers, Duncan pulls a folded half-foolscap sized booklet from his jacket and sets it down.

"Roger Fry gave me this earlier. He believes he's the only gallery owner in England to have received one. Edgar Degas died last September and his collection will now be sold - some of the finest paintings in the world are to be auctioned in ten days' time in Paris. There are pieces he thinks the National Gallery should go for."

Maynard scowls at the catalogue and the accompanying invitation to attend.

'Pastels, Paintings and Drawings belonging to Edgar Degas, from his Studio' it proclaims in bold letters – *'to be Auctioned at the Galerie George Petit, 8 Rue de Seze, March 26th & 27th 1918'*.

Maynard grouchily thumbs his way through the twenty or so pages, making mental notes of the artists and the titles of their works. There would be portraits, landscapes, sketches and studies by Cezanne, Gauguin, Manet, Delacroix, Ingres...

He has to admit, it is a staggering collection. Roger had scribbled some estimated values next to each item and most run into many tens of thousands of francs.

"Certainly prices will be high," confirms Duncan, "but our country should at least *try* to secure some of them even though every art dealer and curator from New York to Naples will be there, including the Scandinavians. Roger told me that a month from now, the French Government will raise taxes on art sales and that this will add to the urgency. He's seeing Charles Holmes, The National's Director, next week to persuade him to go. The Ingres pictures alone would be a most wonderful addition to the collection."

"The National Gallery are in no position to buy anything – their Purchasing Grant was withdrawn when war was declared..." says Maynard, his words trailing off as he continues to stare at the catalogue.

"If we don't get them, someone else will. They'll be dispersed across Europe, disappear into private collections. Or the Germans may steal them and if Paris continues to be bombed, they will be destroyed."

Maynard keeps eating, saying nothing.

"Surely you can finesse something – a Special Grant of some sort?"

Maynard raises his eyebrows then lets them fall again.

"You say that art can be transformative, a force for good for all humankind and that Britain needs such cultural capital – that we must invest in our country as if it's a business. Well now's the chance to use some of those insider skills of yours," says Duncan, still weaponising Maynard's own words against him.

Maynard finally makes eye contact and points a playful finger of mock warning at his friend before pouting, twisting his sensual mouth in that peculiar manner of his then sitting back, putting his hands behind his head, staring, looking at nothing. At the end of his meditation, he nods and affords himself a slight smile before signalling to the waiter to bring on the dessert. Time is passing and they have a train to catch.

In the taxi to Victoria Station, Duncan chats away about Monet's long stay at the Savoy. Like Pissarro, he had fled with his family from France when it was overrun by the Prussian army, finding refuge in London. Duncan talks about the paintings the great man did of Parliament from his hotel room window but Maynard remains much distracted and says little. Only when they turn off Buckingham Palace Road and approach the station forecourt, does he re-engage.

"You're about to meet a new pal of mine" he announces. "He'll be spending the weekend with us…I hope that's alright?"

Duncan is pleased and nods his consent – he understands his friend's need for new company. Maynard has always hated his own appearance, thought himself long, lumpen, beady-eyed and large-lipped. His discomfort in his own body had not been helped by the gentle teasing of his own family or the less-than-affectionate taunting from the other boys at Eton. Although he has been well compensated for these disadvantages by a surfeit of charm and intelligence, his feelings of inadequacy require frequent remedies.

But Duncan too has news. He'd meant to speak of it over dinner but there hadn't been an appropriate moment. Now they were out of time and needs must.

"You'll find things a little changed at Charleston…between Nessa and me."

Maynard frowns.

"We got drunk and it all came out. Now there's no doubt. We are in deepest love." Duncan's eyes moisten and Maynard can feel both his friend's joy and his pain – the fear that it won't last. "It's assuredly from the heart and is really rather wonderful. We have thought she might be pregnant."

Maynard masks his own hurt with a look of happy surprise and places a congratulatory hand on his friend's arm. Duncan is still the ship of his heart but is sailing ever further away.

"I'm most very happy for you, really," says Maynard. "I always knew you had heterosexual tendencies!"

The two friends laugh. The taxi stops. They are arrived.

3

London to Sussex

Victoria Station 1918, Clare Atwood

Although it is almost seven o'clock, inside the station crowds still throng and porters criss-cross with suitcases and trolleys piled high with luggage. After the rarefied atmospheres of *Omega* and the Savoy and the dark quiet of their taxi cab, the yells, whistles, screechings, smoke and hissing steam of a London terminus on a Friday evening are an assault on the senses. Both men recoil with the grimaces of prim ascetics who have suddenly found themselves among brawling drunks on the Old Kent Road.

On the platforms and concourses, troops in uniform are everywhere. A hundred walking-wounded are being guided towards the exit by *Green Cross* girls from the Women's Reserve Royal Ambulance Corps whilst beside an improvised station buffet table, a dozen infantrymen stand drinking tea and smoking. It looks as if a *Leave Train* has just deposited them there and Maynard notices that their steel helmets, gas masks, rucksacks and rifles still hang around their bodies as if this equipment on which their very survival depends in the killing fields of Flanders cannot not be put down for fear of losing it. Their rough jackets and Scottish-style bonnet caps are of regulation khaki and their legs wrapped from ankle to knee in *puttees*, the standard issue bandage-like bindings essential in keeping battlefield filth at bay whether on foot or horseback. The group chat together cheerfully enough at what would likely be their last meeting before each would make their own way home for a regulation four-day leave. Such happiness though would be tempered by the knowledge that they are now a day closer to returning to the front. Most are in their early twenties yet have the world-weariness and pallor of old men.

Even though Maynard and Duncan are both good pacifists and could not in all conscience stand shoulder-to-shoulder with the bonnie boys in the fighting, the two friends glance at each other guiltily. Should they not at least be driving ambulances or be the stretcher bearers of the wounded?

Maynard knows that thirty per-cent of those on the front lines will end up in battlefield hospitals and that another thirty per-cent will be despatched to an eternal rest. All who survive will be forever changed. He keeps his eyes fixed on the ground in front of him as they hurry away, the thump of his ignominious footsteps jarring through his body.

He purchases his weekend return from a First Class ticket window and together, he and Duncan push their way through the sea of travellers to the warm sanctuary of the First Class waiting room. In contrast to the din and mayhem outside, its privileged occupants repose in a polite First Class hush. From the far side of the room, Maynard's new friend spots him and beckons them over.

"This is Georg," says Maynard, as soon as the men are within greeting distance. "…in his final year at Cambridge, reading History,"

"How very apposite. You must explain to me how the world has ended up in such a bloody mess," Duncan says with a half-smile as the introductions are concluded. "Or is recent history not your period?"

Georg wears his hair unfashionably, almost foppishly long, and on the bench beside him rests a dressy fedora hat. The rest of his clothes are, oddly, those of a young fogey – a brown County-tweed suit, a white shirt and blue-red striped college tie. As he studies him again, Maynard sees an impressionable boy who has yet to make proper sense of the world or himself. His cool dispassionate eyes, gaunt features and pale skin convey the ethereal quality of one who has never displayed, probably never even felt, much emotion. There are too few lines of expression on his face.

Georg is not cowed by Duncan's challenging introduction and replies with the fearless self-confidence common amongst Cambridge undergraduates.

"I would be most happy to Mr Grant but…"

"Duncan, please."

"Thank you…Duncan…but such an explanation would take longer than a single weekend in Sussex."

"Perhaps then you will simplify it for me, I'm just a humble painter after all."

"He means of pictures, not of walls and windows frames," says Maynard. All three laugh, earthing some of the static of rivalry and mutual suspicion. The conversation moves on to more amusing pleasantries – student life in Cambridge, the strangeness of the weather and of the people in the surrounding fen country, the London Symphony Orchestra's recent concert at the Queens Hall there in London and the ambition of Nessa's work on the gardens at Charleston. Georg tells them he had visited Gertrude Jekyll's house at Munstead Wood last summer. They continue in this light vein for fifteen minutes before making their way to Platform Six and the Lewes train.

The locomotive stands restlessly puffing away, awaiting the guard's green departure flag and they climb aboard one of the *London, Brighton and South*

Coast Railway's brand new, copper-brown painted, First Class carriages via an end door. They make their way along the corridor to an empty compartment then all three throw their suitcases onto the luggage racks and sink into the soft *Moquette* seats. The train pulls out and clatters across Vauxhall Bridge and before they reach Clapham Junction, they have settled into their cigars and newspapers. After half-an-hour though, just past Caterham Junction, Duncan resolves to find out more about Maynard's new young man. The fellow would after all be spending the weekend with them and it is only good manners to get to know one's house guests even if it would probably be the first and last time he would see him. Maynard's reputation for fast turnovers is well known.

"So how did you two meet?" asks Duncan. His eyes dart between their faces, looking for signs; indications of which one of them is the keener.

"Through John Buchan, at *The Other Club*," answers Maynard, looking up from his copy of *The Times*.

"Not at Cambridge then?"

"I've only returned there to see my mother and not gone at all into College. Besides, Georg isn't at Kings and so we'd never have bumped into each other. And that would have been a tragedy," says Maynard, smiling contentedly at his new partner in sexual crime.

"And tell me more about your studies," Duncan goes on, trying to wrest the young fellow's gaze away from Maynard.

"After I finish my degree, I plan to undertake a D.Phil. I'm examining the proposition that modern civilisation will decline and fall. As you clearly believe the world has gone mad, I think you would find it interesting," says Georg with a smug smile and a terse, clipped delivery. "We expect that just as in ancient Egypt, Greece and Rome, there will be a European slide into *Caesarism* – politics led by the cult of personality and Dictatorship," he continues, setting out his thesis unasked for. "Aristotle foresaw the rise of oligarchies and we believe that they will overwhelm and supercede democracy; due not to national interest nor economic factors but as the result of an inevitable 'change of phase' – like an organism metamorphosing into a different, superior life form. Evolution if you will."

Maynard raises an eyebrow of disapproval in Duncan's direction but does not gainsay his young friend's proposition.

"We therefore think that the fate of the west is sealed. Some believe that Germany under the Kaiser already carries the seeds of the next great dictatorship, that Bolshevism may yet become such a regime. A group has been founded in Italy known as the *Fasces*. They will soon ride a wave of romanticised, heroic, popular mobilisation under some charismatic, authoritarian leader. Professor Spengler at the University of Munich has proven the veracity of these ideas to my satisfaction. My tutor at Emmanuel regularly exchanges essays and ideas with him."

"A Cambridge Don working with the Germans? I'd keep quiet about that if I were you!" warns Duncan light-heartedly.

"The pursuit of knowledge should be unconstrained by national division or temporary conflict - academic research is the unencumbered search for the truth."

"Well said!" exclaims a proud Maynard.

"And just how do their letters move back and forth in the middle of a war?" asks Duncan.

"Some channels remain open. One is through my uncle, he works in the Chancellors' Office with Mr Law. Maynard knows him I think. Our family were from Austria originally and so that has helped."

"You're sure your tutor isn't a spy?!" says Duncan with a grin. He is joking of course but Georg doesn't smile.

Maynard is about to speak when the train is suddenly jolted sideways as if hitting a loose fish plate on the joint of two misaligned rails. The men exchange worried glances.

"There was a derailment near here, at Buxted, just two years ago," says Duncan unreassuringly. "And before the war, seven died on this line at Stoats Nest with many injured. Now the Germans attack trains and bomb the tracks…"

"Where are we?" says Georg, looking out into the darkness, nervously trying to get his bearings.

"We've just left Three Bridges," Maynard explains. "I should have pointed out the new goods marshalling yards we commissioned. They were built to handle the extra war trains, carrying supplies between London and the south coast."

Duncan catches the note of excitement in his friend's voice. '*We* commissioned', he'd announced with pride in his voice. Maynard is a lynch pin in the war effort and sometimes part of Duncan envies that. The nation's mothers, sisters and daughters now work in armaments factories, others drive ambulances or nurse in battlefield hospitals, some risk spying in dangerous lands. Even the Suffragettes had suspended their campaign in order to support the nation in its hour of need. He thinks too of the 1st Battalion of the Artist's Rifles who on New Years' last, bravely, selflessly, left their trenches to counter-attack. Only twelve from the eighty were spared death or deep wounding. He has seen John Nash's sketches for his painting of the nightmare, *Over the Top*. It will show soldiers dressed in winter greatcoats scrambling from trenches onto a snowy landscape. Seven already lie felled as the others move forward, resolutely not looking back. The dark clouds of deep winter hang threateningly in the sky above.

When he thinks of these things, his own preoccupations seem ridiculous, pitiful and pointless - his paintings the clumsy daubings of a man desperate to be thought of as a great artist, his piss-pathetic attempts to grow a few vegetables a spineless bribe in return for being allowed to conscientiously object. If he were to die tonight, such would be his epitaph.

"It's Haywards Heath next," continues Maynard. "They've put in new passing loops so passenger trains won't get held up by the goods traffic, and they hold munitions trains there too...during air raids. We'll be taking the branch line to Lewes at Keymer Junction."

Then, realising he'd been carried away by his own interests, he turns to Georg and rests his hand on the boy's arm. "I'm sorry, you must be very tired. We're almost there," he says with a reassuring pat.

4

At Charleston Farmhouse

For some unknown reason and against all the blackout regulations, the lights in Lewes Station's ticket hall burn brightly tonight and the normally dim-lit space once again sparkles and sings out its welcome. Maynard knows the building was designed by Thomas Harrison Myers, a devotee of the same style of architecture adopted at Queen Victoria's Osborne House and as they walk through, he pauses once more to enjoy its *Italianate* decoration. Here and in many other stations owned by the *London and Brighton*, classical devices abound – outside, the buff and red brickwork structure is topped with ornate pinnacles and Greek urns and its main roof slopes upwards to a wide, glass-sided clerestory lantern under which a grand chandelier hangs.

"How very wonderful," he says. "What a marvel the railway must have seemed to its first passengers. Every town and city in the land was now theirs for work or pleasure, to be reunited with long unseen relatives or to visit the Great Exhibition in London! A simple train ticket became a passport to walk among your fellow countrymen irrespective of social class and to delight in the grandeur of the great railway termini – the cathedrals of the modern age."

Georg and Duncan also stare about them, smiling at the thought of it.

"And travel with your portable easel and work *plein air* – to paint land and sea in sunlight exactly as it falls," says Duncan.

"All would have felt such optimism," continues Maynard, "that their grandchildren would inherit a nation so full of advancement and possibility…"

But the sudden appearance of a half-dozen unsmiling soldiers in uniform trudging past them on their way to the platforms stops Maynard's celebration in its tracks. He shakes his head and frowns as he walks towards the station's exit. The others know what he is thinking.

The three men had left the train in a casual manner but once outside, they quickly regret their sloth. There isn't a cab in sight and a queue of ten has already formed. Not even horse and carriage are on offer. It is now eight forty-five on a cold, drizzly Friday evening and prolonged discomfort and inconvenience looks likely. But whilst Duncan slouches sullenly against the station wall and Georg begins to fret, Maynard swings into action.

"Wait here for fifteen minutes then stand over by that wall" he says quietly, gesturing like a conspirator towards the far side of the station forecourt. "I shall meet you there."

Duncan nods his agreement as Maynard turns and strides purposefully off in the direction of the town's High Street. Whatever his friend is up to, Duncan knows it will work. At the fifteen minute mark he and Georg take up their positions and almost immediately, headlamps appear through the River Ouse mist and a chugging taxi draws up. Maynard throws open the door and beckons them to jump inside.

"The porter at the White Hart Hotel always keeps at least one driver on standby, to ferry guests around," he says as his friends clamber in. "If any cabs are free, he's usually happy to accommodate me. It is an arrangement of mutual benefit," he adds with a wink.

The driver hops out to load their bags onto the open-sided luggage deck and Duncan and Georg fall back into their seats with grateful sighs. In the dark of the taxi, feelings of great relief settle on the three men as their talk turns to the weekend's planned itinerary of pleasure at Charleston, now just seven miles away to the east.

Twenty minutes later, the taxi drops them at the end of Charleston's unmade lane and with stretched strides and side-steps to avoid the mud, they advance slowly towards the houselights. Rising steeply up behind the farm, the black mass of Firle Beacon sits atop the South Downs towering seven hundred feet above them. Beyond those grass-covered chalk hills and Neolithic burial barrows is the coast at Newhaven and the English Channel. Maynard hopes that tomorrow, if there is time and opportunity, he and Georg will walk its cliff paths to take-in lungful's of ocean air and be madly smitten with each other. He crosses his fingers that they will not hear the distant boom of Flanders' guns rolling in across the water.

Duncan pushes open Charleston's front door and calls out that he is home. Now Maynard silently prays to the god of all agnostics that this weekend, the place would once more be bathed in the soft light of happiness, that things would be as they once were before damnable war and his role in it had divided them. Only Duncan loves him now. Nessa still cares but must battle to keep her disappointment in him in check. Jinny, Lytton, Ottoline, Bunny and the rest, if they are there tonight, would likely gather in other rooms rather than find themselves in further bitter dispute with him.

In the hallway, as they clean the mud from their shoes, Nessa appears, togged in a wide apron covered in spots of paint and food stains, flushed and sweating. Oblivious to the presence of Maynard and Georg, she rushes to Duncan and falls into his arms. What Maynard sees between them is yes, new. They had been friends of course, dear friends, for years and more lately lovers, but it seems now that both are changed. He had noticed something different in his friend as soon as they met today but had been unable to put his finger on it. Now he understands. Duncan's restlessness has, at least in part, found repose.

Nessa's eyes smile with tenderness. As her two young sons tumble into the hall, her manner with them is different also. Love has remade her but unlike ill-fated Juliet, she seems not in conflict with her familial word but more at ease. Where before her children had provoked sharp exasperation or suffocating maternalism, all is now non-judging affection. It occurs to

35

Maynard that she is become protected from the trials of family life by a holy amnion of requited love and that her forbearance of her tousle-haired, anarchic boys has been made infinite. He hopes this new nature of understanding will now be extended to himself.

Introductions and greetings are conducted with customary Charleston informality. Hugs are exchanged and cheeks kissed but the starchy Georg is horribly uncomfortable with such displays of emotion and remains expressionless throughout his ordeal. Once coats are removed and bags deposited at the foot of the stairs, Nessa clasps her hands together and takes a deep breath. She has an announcement to make and instructions to issue.

"My husband is not here. He has left for Brighton with someone named Bella who is, he tells me, Hungarian. Jinny and Bunny are in London."

The three men stand wearing passive smiles, like officers waiting for orders from a general.

"Maynard should take the bags upstairs whilst Duncan and Georg come into the kitchen with me. Duncan can finish cooking supper whilst Georg tells me all about himself and how he got tangled up with the bookkeeper of our nation's war criminals. We're still angry with him," she says, turning to Georg, "but I'm sure he's already told you about that."

"No, not really…" says the lad, his nervousness revealing itself in the tight smile now on his face. Maynard winces but gives Georg a reassuring wink and gestures to him to follow the departing Nessa into the back of the house.

All of the rooms in decrepit, rambling Charleston are filled with art. All of the rooms *are* art. Many oils and sketches are hung on the walls of course but others are leant, stacked or rolled up in corners. Easels and palettes are everywhere. But in this house, art does not stop at the edge of a picture frame. Ceilings, fire surrounds, mantle shelves, door frames and architraves; all are covered in swirls of coloured figures and geometric designs – everyday fixtures and fittings have been honoured to receive the loving attentions of Nessa and Duncan and their artist guests who wish to lift the nation's houses from the mundane to the beautiful. Outside, Maynard knows the gardens are full of sculpture.

Their late supper that evening might have been basic to the taste but it too is a feast for the eyes. An orange and green root vegetable stew with bright yellow dumplings is so lurid in hue that Maynard wonders if Nessa or Grace, her cook, had added food colouring. He exchanges a knowing look with Duncan confirming the wisdom of his decision to have eaten at The Savoy before they set off. That would likely be the last normal meal Maynard would get all weekend. But he wouldn't grumble, food supplies in this remote part of wartime Sussex were limited and Nessa had done her best as she always did.

Her sons, Julian and Quentin, are allowed to eat with them and to stay up as long as they please. They are lovely boys and Maynard is well used to them but their presence means that for a full hour, the conversation

37

concerns the challenges of building garden dens with leafless branches in March and Julian's disputed claim to have spotted both a butterfly and a moth last week when the weather warmed a little. By ten-thirty though, the children are fading and of their own accord, leave the table to the three adults.

After dinner, over more wine and cognac, it isn't long before talk becomes philosophical debate and politics. Personal Politics. As Maynard would say, 'is there any other kind?' The dining table quickly transforms into a battlefield as for Nessa's benefit, Duncan summarises Georg's view of history, of the inexorability of western civilisation's decline, just as he had set out on the train journey down. But this time, Maynard, freed-up by Friday night conviviality and its accompanying alcoholic lubricants, proves a combative counter-weight.

"So you have been persuaded that even once peace is achieved, democracy is still doomed?" enquires Maynard, as he lights a cigar and looks inquisitorially into Georg's boyish face.

"Yes, it is Europe's inevitable destiny, pre-ordained by human greed and distrust."

"I cannot believe we have come so far only to fail," says Maynard, now with a look of utmost seriousness. It is as if a switch has been flicked and he is changed from jaunty conversationalist to statesman.

"An equitable sharing of the common wealth, healing medicines, mechanicals used for good… these things will forge a new collective happiness. The fate of nations is neither grim nor immutable – it lies in the hands of the people and in the hearts of leaders touched by the angels of their better selves."

"Please forgive our evangelistic friend. He strives constantly to save the world from itself," says Duncan with an impish grin.

"A hazard of being the son of a Baptist father and a social reformer mother," replies Maynard, with a wide smile. "But you are right to be suspicious. God save us from the goody-goody gang, the busybodies, spoilsports and piously high-minded who tell everyone else what to think. That is religion, not politics, and here's to free thought!"

Maynard raises his glass in a mock toast as Duncan and Nessa chuckle but Georg looks on, perplexed.

"Georg, my dear, whatever your studies may have taught you, we must never look back in despair but ever forward with hope," Maynard continues. "My grandfather was 'in trade', a plantsman who became successful enough to buy his children a good schooling. And so here I am, the inheritor of that vision of better times, the fulfilment of his dreams, a Cambridge man and now privy to the great affairs of State. The absence of poverty, education and artistic beauty are the antidotes to self-interest, suppression and fear and we will be their purveyors. These remedies are our shield against Aristotle's oligarchs."

"This is but fantasy – I thought you a scholar of history, a man of logic?" says Georg.

"I am those things, yes" replies Maynard, "but scholarship will show you that few men can judge matters by anything other than the conditions of their own times. The classical world's harbingers of doom could not have imagined non-slave societies or universal literacy and suffrage. Socrates and Plato would not have foreseen the part which will be played by civilisation's emancipated women, and how they will change the world."

"The weaker gender, leading the way? You jest surely!"

Nessa bridles but says nothing, she knows well the tragedy of the closed-minded male. It is the defensiveness of the fearful and the weak and just as a drowning man might fight off attempts to save him, argument is wasted on such people until they are ready to hear it.

"The evidence is already here to be seen," answers Maynard. "Is not Dora Carrington a better artist than either Duncan or Roger, Jinny Wolff a more original writer than both Lytton and Bunny, Nessa, a more creative thinker than her husband? Many women will make fine leaders, unlike most of us men."

"My friend is, I hate to admit, quite right," says Duncan, proudly smiling at Nessa as he leans across to squeeze her hand.

Maynard now sits upright in his chair, like a judge preparing himself for his final summing up.

"Our community of friends here is the harvest of the best of mankind's intentions and the beauty it creates will be its legacy. We have our trials and tribulations, of course – we are a prototype. But all are equal and honest and such democracy is hard," he says, relighting his cigar. "It is though most worthy of our best efforts."

He inhales more smoke and knocks back another mouthful of brandy.

"Now, what about a game of Bridge?" he says, his relaxed congeniality now fully restored.

Duncan and Nessa seem keen but Georg looks down at his empty glass and says nothing. He stays silent for a few seconds then sheepishly makes his apologies.

"I'm sorry, I think I might go to bed. I'm terribly tired."

Goodnights are exchanged as Georg stands up and departs. The three friends pass around more smokes and drink and wait for their guest to be out of earshot.

"He'll be thinking that ever since first you met, you've just been humouring him…" says Duncan in hushed tones.

"Perhaps I have, yes, but I've heard his bleak prophecies many times before. They are well-argued of course, but are for the consumption of ivory-towered, non-participating observers. We activists cannot afford to think such things," says Maynard. "But whatever the truth of it, I fear the copulation tonight will be less than enthusiastic."

All three laugh but Maynard realises that Georg would have heard their raucousness and rightly concluded that the amusement was at his expense. The sex will now most definitely be off the menu.

The kitchen table is cleared and the two men quickly swing into action washing and drying plates as Nessa lights up another cigarette.

"Duncan has shown me the catalogue for the Degas sale," she says, inhaling a lungful of the sweet smoke. "Can you not persuade your accomplices at the Treasury to give the National Gallery a small loan to buy even one or two? The public must be allowed to see them."

"I've already told her it's impossible," says Duncan. "The prices at the auction will be sky-high and we're in the middle of a war. Try telling our MPs and a boorish all-male electorate that buying art is a good use of public funds."

Maynard pauses his domestic duties, saying nothing for five portentous seconds. "I think I'll put these pans into soak before doing anything more," he finally says, before manipulating his stiff lower back with those long, bony fingers of his. Duncan and Nessa know their friend well and wait for him to continue.

"Firstly, I don't think you should be so hard on the British voter," he says. "Families have been impoverished. Some have lost the sons they were counting on to provide for them in old age and thousands of long-term wounded will never work again. Most of the electorate would not see why spending the country's money at an art auction in Paris was a good idea."

Still Nessa and Duncan say nothing.

"Second, prices at the Degas sale will be low, not high."

"But hundreds of bidders will be there, from all over the world," Duncan protests. "Your supply and demand curve will be almost vertical; the sums astronomical."

Maynard turns and smiles at his friend's grasp of this basic principle of economics, then is once again straight-faced.

"A great deal of information comes across my desk, military as well as economic. I have to tell you, most secretly, that our generals think the war will now intensify. Peace with Russia has freed up the German armies in the east and by the summer, American troops will have arrived in force and be actively engaged on our side. Now is Germany's best chance, some think their last chance, for victory. If there is increased ferocity in France, many art buyers will be deterred. The supply and demand curve is now a lot flatter, yes?"

Duncan nods, but as he acknowledges his friend's logic, his mind fills with pictures of a bloody hell, the toll a new murderous wave of attacks will exact. *L'actualité.* He sees the muddied corpses – the farm labourers and gardeners, the bookkeepers, butchers boys and shop assistants, teachers and thatchers. The bodies of the village lads dismembered, scarlet clods of flesh and bone scattered across the fields like the devil's fertiliser, making ready the ground for more seeds of hatred. He closes his eyes at the horror of it all but is mercifully brought back by Maynard's strong voice.

"We think that Roger's catalogue is the only one in Britain and in all likelihood it will be the same across Europe," he says, "Galerie Petit's invitations may have been lost on-route. That's to our advantage, and even those who know of the auction may not come – they'd have to skirt the battlefields then get their precious booty home again through the chaos of war. Railways are destroyed, the Channel ports are bombed, borders are closed and many roads around Paris are cratered. Buyers will not be able to carry the paintings home on their backs, they're rather bulky you know."

"But what of the French galleries, the Louvre, they will bid against you surely?" asks Nessa.

"They'll have the same problem we do – their populace won't like the idea of spending monies on art when there are shortages of food. Civil unrest waits in the wings. Some there fear another revolution."

"So great art will languish in Paris until the Germans either destroy it or carry it back to Berlin like Sabine women – to be sold as spoils of war into private collections. We are all of us but trustees of the world's wonders and must save them for the future."

"A problem is an opportunity in disguise," says Maynard, smugly. Duncan and Nessa look confused but intrigued. What card has their clever friend got up his sleeve?

"Our National Gallery's purchasing grant was withdrawn at the start of the war so they'll get no more money to spend here in England. But as Head of External Finance, how the British Government defines *overseas* expenditure is up to me. Any money we spend in France helps their economy and therefore counts as a war loan but instead of their worthless IOUs, we'll get the art."

He picks up his glass of cognac and takes another gulp, belching as the warm nectar enters his stomach.

"There'll be rather more to it than that but you can leave those Heuristic machinations to me. You tell me what to buy and I'll concoct the ways to pay for it. We'll restock the nation's art collection and the viewing of it will be shared by all our people, rich and poor alike."

"The Chancellor is a Philistine and Lloyd George too. Why would they and their cronies agree to it?" asks Nessa.

"Because they can't afford to let an opportunity like this pass them by – to get French art at bargain prices from under the noses of an invading German army! We have ways in and out of Paris the Germans do not yet know of or can threaten," he says, conspiratorially tapping the side of his nose. "What a coup it would be, what a brave adventure, what a vote-winner! Trust me, it's too mouth-watering a prospect for them to resist."

Nessa and Duncan look at each other and smile.

"And for my part, it is the Ides of March today – in ancient Rome, the deadline for settling all debts," says Maynard. "Dear friends, I owe you much, but I owe my country everything."

5

The Game Begins

Everyone is awake by seven o'clock the following morning. Well, almost everyone. Even after a night of erotic inertia, Georg remains soundly asleep. As Maynard dresses, he determines to return to London, with or without his new friend. Outside his bedroom window, the spring sun lights up the budding garden and fills him with enthusiasm for the days ahead. But the imminence of the auction means there is no time to lose. He must start his Degas endeavours today.

Over a breakfast of sweet black tea, salted herring, eggs and homemade bread, whilst Maynard is his usual ebullient self, Duncan and Nessa ease more slowly into the day. Last night's planning of the Degas coup had been as intense and exhausting as it was exciting and at times she leans a tired head on his shoulder.

Though it had been well into the early hours and all three had been more than a little tipsy, Nessa had been quite clear on which works in the collection were must-buys and had written out a list, ranked according to desirability. There would be twenty in all including two by Manet and Delacroix, one each by Gauguin, Corot, Rousseau, Cezanne and Ricard and no less than eleven by Ingres. She said that if Maynard pulled this off, it would finally justify his dubious presence at the Treasury adding that it was his bounden duty and that he could not, must not fail. She had told him also that the involvement of Roger Fry would be pivotal to the mission's success – that he would know the right people in Paris to accompany the National Gallery's buyers at the sale and that the auction crowd would be full of foreign tricksters. He must be wary.

After breakfast, they leave the clearing up to the housekeeper, dress in warm coats and stroll in the garden among the hens and ducks who, like Nessa's children, are free to roam wherever they wish. It has been a month since Maynard's last visit and even though much of nature remains dormant, the pond with its overhanging Willow tree and the borders and beds are in good repair and ready for the growth to come. The place is no Garsington but flint and stone walls have been restored and the orchard trees are pruned and they talk of how Nessa's efforts and those of her gardeners will bear real fruit this year. The three friends are happy and even in these despairing days of war, it seems to them that there is much to live for. Then Maynard clouds the sky of their sunny Saturday.

"I am minded to return to London this morning," he says. Nessa and Duncan slow their steps, waiting to hear his reasons.

"If we are to carry out our Degas coup, I must now write to our many unsuspecting abetters, send telegrams, make telephone calls…there is much which requires careful consideration. Once I'm at my Monday desk, daily matters will demand my attention and allow neither the time nor the space of mind to plan our scheme in the detail it needs. I am sorry."

Though Duncan is saddened, Nessa nods her approval.

"We shall miss your company but yes, of course, go with our blessing," she says, squeezing his arm.

Maynard pauses for a second, choosing his words carefully before taking her hand in his.

"I would have the Director of the National Gallery accompany me to Paris. It must be he who attends for no one else can verify the provenance and merit of the works. We shall need such authority in order to release the monies."

Duncan and Nessa stop in their tracks.

"You will go yourself?" says Nessa. "My dear, it's out of the question. You'd have to cross the Somme battlefields and you said yourself that the city could be under siege."

"It's too dangerous Maynard. You can't go, not even for beauty's sake," pleads Duncan, shaking his head.

"The Treasury will insist that one of its staff is there to oversee the purchases – I calculate we shall need in the region of twenty-thousand pounds. And if anyone else goes they would most assuredly make a pig's fuck of it. As luck would have it, I shall be in Paris anyway – the Inter-Allied Finance Council will meet there at the very same time as the auction."

"What Council?" she says, a little coldly. "And what does it do, devise cheaper ways of burying the war dead?"

Duncan frowns and taps her arm as if counselling forbearance.

"It's a monkey house, a cage of brutes...American bankers securing more profit on their loans to the allies...decisions made for reasons of political self-interest. I have told you many times, I am working for a Government I despise for ends I think are criminal. But rather me than someone less well-intentioned," he says, still trying to prize-out some sort of approval from her.

"If you deal with the devil, he will steal your soul" she replies, as sceptical as ever.

"And if you don't deal with him, someone else will. I can win," he says cheerily, "beat him because I have engineered his underestimation of me. I know his desires but he does not know mine. His lusts are always the same, he is therefore utterly predictable. I can outplay him."

Nessa shrugs, unconvinced. She thinks the devil will always find ways to subvert good intentions.

"Well let's hope the devils on this Paris Council of yours don't hear about our Degas sale," Duncan says, moving the conversation on. "I'm sure they're every bit as wily as you are."

"The men on the Council with me will be on the lookout for good wines and wicked women, not great art," says Maynard.

Duncan laughs but Nessa stays glum. She is putting on a brave show but her furrowed brow shows that her fears for Maynard's safety remain.

"And I've not told you, it is another secret," adds Maynard, seeing her concern. "This Council has already made the journey to Paris three times in the last twelve months. A military escort is provided for the duration. I will be safe."

"A platoon of soldiers won't stop bombs, torpedoes or sea mines," mutters Duncan with a shake of his head.

There is another silence as the three friends dwell on the thought of the worst that could happen.

"Shall we go inside now?" says Maynard, giving Nessa a final pat on the arm. She grips his hand as if a terrible fear has come over her. If something were to happen to him, she would blame herself.

Inside Charleston once more, Maynard goes upstairs to gather up the last of his things and finds Georg still in the process of regaining consciousness. He leans down and kisses him on the cheek.

"I must return to London. Something's come up."

"That's more than's happened here," says Georg, sleepily.

"Sorry. We'll try again another time."

Georg doesn't answer.

"You're most welcome to stay for the rest of the weekend, I've squared it with Duncan and Nessa – they'd be thrilled to have you."

"They might be but I'm not. I find them rather unintelligent and more than a little mad. Like many of the crowd you've introduced me to, they're self-obsessed and indulgent and use pacifism as a pretence for getting out of going to war. I shall be relocating to Hove."

"I must meet *your* friends sometime."

Georg stays silent.

"On second thoughts, perhaps not," says Maynard before leaving the room without saying goodbye, closing the door firmly behind him.

On the train back up to town, the plans for his Degas coup begin to coalesce and by the time he sits down at his desk in the evening stillness of his rooms in Gordon Square, he can see their fine grain. Like one of his beloved mathematical proofs, he formulates a series of connected steps, the logic of each he now re-checks.

First, he will enthuse Charles Holmes, the head of The National Gallery, assuring him of the merits and feasibility of the project. Maynard knows that his position as Director is not what it once was and that the incumbent no longer has the absolute power to buy whatever they want. Now, with his wings clipped, Holmes has set his sights on expanding the Gallery's educative purposes, wishing to produce a series of explanatory catalogues whilst adding less well-known pictures which show the History of European Art. It is their excellent good fortune that Nessa's list of desired acquisitions is perfectly in accord with this new ambition and Maynard will convince Holmes that getting Treasury money to buy some of the Degas hoard is not only possible but actually rather easy. Holmes will surely take the bait. Yes, he will.

Next, Maynard will corner Lord Curzon; well-connected Member of Parliament, Chairman of the Gallery's Trustees, and explain that French painters of this period – Delacroix, Ingres and the rest, are unrepresented at Trafalgar Square and therefore urgently needed to complete the national collection.

'My Lord, all England will applaud your vision, future generations will bless your name,' he will tell him. It will be an easy sell.

Then he must take the plan to Chalmers and Meiklejohn, his seniors at the Treasury, and with their support in place, explain to the Chancellor that instead of getting worthless French IOUs for the money we were lending to them, Britain would get the paintings instead. A cynic would call this Creative Accounting but it will be plausible enough to forearm Curzon so that he can head-off any awkward questions in Parliament. Step One will then be complete.

Step Two will involve arranging for the British Embassy in Paris to have 'Special Grant' monies ready in their account so that cheques can be signed at the Degas sale. With the Chancellor of the Exchequer's authorisation in his pocket and the Director of the National Gallery at his side to carry out the purchases, Maynard will travel to Paris to attend the next meeting of the International Finance Commission – the Inter-Ally Council, but will also go to the auction. He and Holmes will slip away and attend the sale incognito and easily outbid the few other collectors in attendance. How satisfying it will be.

Step Three will involve getting out of war-torn Paris unmolested and travelling close to the battlefields of the Somme with twenty fragile, cumbersome oil paintings, hoping to avoid enemy gunfire. They must then sail across a mine-filled English Channel, patrolled by German warships and submarines, before getting the precious cargo safely home by train to the National Gallery on tracks frequently bombed by Hun aeroplanes.

Though he sits alone in his study, Maynard laughs out loud at the recklessness of it all. The whole thing is quite mad. Success is possible but hardly probable. The Theory cannot be proven correct, the plan is flawed, undone by risk factors of great vector. Damn. Blast.

But securing outrageous profit requires the acceptance of commensurably long odds against success does it not? Only high risk yields high reward. He is suddenly surprised, delighted by his own fortitude. He remembers his Cambridge days, The Apostles' group of young thinkers, G.E. Moore's revelatory *Principia Ethica*. These things have instilled in him a fearlessness, a realisation that he could create his own myth and make it real. He will throw off the shackles of the adversity and seize the day. He would succeed in this venture and the ungainly, ugly, wife-less outsider, the grandson of tradesmen will be raised up high. He has a picture of himself which he would now come to be. His mother will be proud and his friends would love him again. Though full of danger, his Degas coup will be comprised of logical, easy-to-follow steps and is morally, aesthetically, financially, the right thing to do. *Quod Erat Demonstrandum.*

6

Holmes and Fry

Before opening the *Omega Workshops* in 1913, Roger Fry had been an editor of art periodicals, a critic, the curator at the Metropolitan Museum of Art in New York. He is still a working artist.

Eight years ago he took the risk to introduce the Post-Impressionists – Gauguin, Cezanne, Seurat and Van Gogh, to the London art world and probably wished he hadn't bothered. Accused of being a subverter of public morals as well as of Fine Art, some detractors had even invoked his wife's precarious mental state as a way to ridicule him further. But the genie of Modern Art was out of the bottle and as Nessa's sister Virginia Woolf had said at the time, "on the day that exhibition opened in December 1910, human character changed."

Roger has a face of sharp intelligence – a little hawk-featured perhaps but full of humour just waiting to escape. Although there had been the inevitable in-fighting among the cooperative members of *Omega*, it had overall been a happy project and it is here, at 33 Fitzroy Square in his upstairs studio, that Fry and Holmes meet on the Tuesday morning after Maynard's visit to Charleston.

Charles John Holmes, Director of the National Gallery – painter, academic, art historian and critic; is forty-nine years old and has kindly eyes and a broad, high forehead. Since his days at Eton and Oxford, he had tried many things, achieved much, but never greatness as an artist. His work is competent, exhibitions have been given, including at the Venice Biennale, and pictures sold, but in the years past spent researching the Old Masters – Raphael, El Greco and the rest, he grew to realise that his painterly abilities were of the commonplace category. He has peered many times into the chasm between genius and mere craft and knows that the bridging of such a gap, even if possible, is most hazardous. With no guarantee of success, every waking hour must be spent in such an enterprise, hanging high above the abyss, buffeted by scarifying winds, with downfall never more than an ill-judged step away. So in place of sacrifice, he has instead chosen comfort – family, friends and days spent in the study of those who had bravely chosen to risk everything to become Great, to be the instruments of God. He tells himself that the curation and stewardship of the works of others fulfils a valuable function, that it is a worthy calling. It is something is it not? Yes, it is much.

He and Roger have been friends for years and mutual acceptance of their own limitations as artists is an unspoken bond between them. Today, they are consoled by the knowledge that few know as much about the techniques of Renaissance Florentine art as they and that none, in England at least, understand its meanings better.

"So, might you be interested?" asks Fry.

He and Holmes stand looking down on a painting of just ten inches by eight as it lays flat on a draughtsman's table illuminated by a single lamp. *The Adoration of the Shepherds* dated from around 1480 and used egg tempera, not oil, as the medium, the binder, for the coloured pigments applied to its thin Cedarwood board. It is a biblical scene from the life of Christ which had inspired at least thirty other interpretations including those by El Greco, Rubens and the belligerent, brawling, murderous Caravaggio.

The little painting shows two ragged-arsed peasants standing in respectful awe as they look down upon the holy infant and his mother. The baby lies in a wicker crib on the floor of a stable with a ruined wall on one side and the fortified city of Jerusalem in the far distance, portentously showing Christ's ultimate destination. His father Joseph, yellow cloaked with wooden staff in hand, stares down with a morose expression of resignation as if knowing his son is destined to tread a stony path whetted by hard rain and tears.

"The attribution concerns me," says Holmes. "Is it really a Parentino? It may be by Butinone. The *Bolletino dell'Arte* suggests he can be confused with others at the school of Ferrara."

"That's because Mantegna taught one of them and influenced the other. Either way, it won't affect the value. Both are of unquestionable high-status."

"That uncertainty will make the Trustees nervous and even once our purchasing grant is restored, they may block us. If I recommend its acquisition and other panels from the original Lombardino altarpiece turn up and are shown to be Butinones, I shall look very foolish."

"My dear chap, you should know by now that looking foolish is part and parcel of being a curator. Being 'had' – tricked, lied to, misled and at times in error, is inevitable."

"The Trustees of the National Gallery remain determinedly unphilosophical regarding bad judgment. Your first mistake is your last. There's as much politicking at Trafalgar Square as there is in Parliament Square – there are many who would be happy to see me fail."

"I am worried about you my friend, you have become care-worn and cautious – like an old man," Fry sighs, "let us leave this for another day." He is exasperated but experienced enough to know that his friend is in truth nibbling at the bait. He would reel him in sooner or later.

Roger picks up the disputed painting by its corners and gestures to Holmes to follow him into the small glass-walled office next to the studio. He lays the piece down on a table in the corner, covers it in a cream-coloured muslin wrap then walks back across the room and closes the door tight shut.

"Have you seen this?" he says, going to his desk and pushing the Degas catalogue in Holmes' direction. "I would be surprised if you had. As far as I know, I'm the only person in England to have received one."

Holmes picks up the small, book-sized brochure and slides down into a leather armchair next to the window, his relaxed body language immediately beginning to stiffen as his eyes move across the pages. Within five seconds, he is sitting bolt upright, straining to find the best light by which to read the list of great works he can hardly believe he is seeing.

"So the old bastard had all of this hoarded away?" says Holmes, in awe. "You knew him didn't you?"

"Yes. And everything they said about Edgar was true – he was a bad-tempered, anti-Semitic misanthropist."

"Well no-one's perfect," quips Holmes.

Fry smiles.

"But he was a very great artist," he adds.

Roger reclines back in his chair and half-closes his eyes, recalling Degas' genius. "Yes, the maker of so many wonderful things," he says dreamily. "The dancers, the nudes – such movement! And the use of colour...I hadn't appreciated the real magic of pastels until he took to me to Roche's shop where he bought them. Almost all are pure pigment with minimal binders added – the Ultra Marine Blue, Brilliant Pink, Cadmium Yellow..."

Roger drifts for a few seconds in silent, heavenly reverie before returning to *terra firma*. "But there's little of his own work for sale this at this auction – the executors are holding it back for some reason," he says, filling his pipe. "Degas was a very difficult man but one forgives him. He once said that art was not what you see but what you make others see, and he saw much in the work of others. He collected some of the finest works ever made and on the 26th of March, that's a week today, we can buy some of it. Or rather the Gallery can, the National Gallery. You can..." Roger's words trail off as a small smile starts to play around the corners of his mouth. It is as if he already knows how the conversation will end even if his unsuspecting friend does not.

Holmes' eyebrows furrow. He is just about to remind them both that the National has no money, and what is more, no prospect of any until the war's end when Roger dives back in.

"Maynard Keynes was here last evening on the pretext of returning this catalogue and to give me a ticking-off for breaking an appointment with some young printmaker. But what he really wanted was to explain his new plan, he calls it his *Degas Coup*. He thinks we should buy some of the best works from this auction for our National Gallery, that the paintings will educate your visitors and enrich the nation's culture and the Treasury too."

Roger then excitedly explains how the raid would work, how the money would be in the form of a Special Grant, written-off against French war loans, and that Holmes had to now write to Lord Curzon, the Chief Trustee of the National Gallery, to get his support.

"Maynard believes that because he's an MP, Curzon is the bridge which will take us across the sea of squabbling objection straight into the Chancellor's Office. The final sign-off to release the monies will be Bonar Law's of course but the worst that can happen is that he'll say 'no'."

"Wrong. The worst that can happen is he'll think I'm stark staring mad for supporting such an idea and have me sacked."

But Holmes now feels increasingly powerless, a weak-willed fool being drawn inexorably out of his depth, a reluctant accomplice in the schemes of others.

"And just what exactly would Maynard have me write in this letter?" he asks.

"He's drafted it out for you – all you have to do is copy it, sign it and send it. It makes the case admirably and explains each part of the plan in just the right amount of detail. Assuming you and he make it to Paris in one piece, we think twenty-thousand pounds should be enough for a decent haul," says Roger, handing Holmes the letter. "Maynard and I finalised the list last night, taking account of Nessa Bell's and Duncan's suggestions. We need an Ingres portrait – I've been after one since my days in New York – and we want Delacroix and Manet, and a Corot too if possible? These works will show the British public the beginnings of Modern art, the origins of Impressionism. There's little of it on display anywhere else in the country. We've included a Gauguin and a Cezanne too but I know these later works may be more difficult to get Curzon's approval for. You can only try."

"And who from the National will go to Paris with Maynard?"

"We're all of the same mind as to what to buy but I'd be interested to see if you agree," says Roger, ignoring the question. "The final decision will be yours of course so please, add in anything you believe should be gone after. There's a notepad on the desk."

"You do realise that twenty thousand pounds is one hundred times the British annual working wage?"

"And so?"

"And so the public will never stand for it."

"The public will never know – not until the war's over anyway. We must all 'seal our lips and give no words but mum'. Oh, and Maynard thinks you should go in disguise. At the very least, shave off your moustache."

Holmes' mouth falls open. *He* was to go to Paris? Cross an English Channel of sea mines and enemy submarines and skirt battlefields of artillery and sniper fire?

"If word gets out the National Gallery is going to the auction, Maynard thinks prices will go up," says Fry, "and the Louvre's buyers will be compelled to outbid you just to save face. To them, the British have neither the education nor the sensibilities to appreciate great art let alone be the fit custodians of it."

Holmes' head is spinning but he knows now that he is duty bound to go. Roger may be right, perhaps it will do him good – shake him out of his current torpor, release him from the drab routine of officialdom. But how he would explain this madness to his wife? She would not understand a man's need to face his own fear, to prove to one's self in a time of war, to show that you were no white-feathered coward. He is not even sure he understands these things himself but go to Paris he must.

"And a disguise might make things a tad less risky for you personally... physically I mean," adds Fry.

"Sorry, I'm not with you."

"There will be German spies at Boulogne, perhaps even at Folkestone and certainly in Paris. Maynard doesn't want you identified. If they put two and two together, they might try to kill you, sabotage the entire auction or swipe our paintings on the way home through France and if that doesn't work, they'll send you and the paintings to the bottom of the English Channel. It would all be rather embarrassing."

Roger pours out two small brandies and passes one to his friend.

"But let us not fret too much," says Fry, smiling and raising his glass. "I'm sure it will turn out to be a rather tepid, routine sort of affair. Maynard says there is no place in the world for irrational plans, and that beauty is the best test of any theory. He assures me that this Degas coup of his is both logical and beautiful. So here's to our rescue mission – and your mild adventure!"

But Charles Holmes doesn't join his friend in the toast. Instead, he half-smiles and stares silently down at the paint-spattered floor.

7

The Seat of Power

At two forty-five p.m. on Thursday the 21st of March, with just four days to go before the auction, Maynard hurriedly leaves his office in the Treasury building, walks through the hidden Government streets and passage ways of Whitehall and arrives outside the door of number eleven Downing Street. When it is opened, he enters then stands impatiently in a corner before pacing around the parquet-floored hallway, waiting to see Chancellor Bonar Law.

In his mind, the details of his Degas coup compete for space with the residue of today's already attended to duties. Since he'd sat down at his desk at eight this morning, it had been a day of predictable but manic normality. He had drafted memoranda for members of the Cabinet on the loans to Russia, on the current state of Britain's' gold reserves and the progress of his talks with the Americans concerning their help in financing the war. Then, as one of the designers and custodians of the Bank of England's centralised buying system used to control war expenditure, he'd authorised another French purchase of munitions and an invoice for their Italian allies to import a freighter full of luxurious ladies' underwear. He'd been amused to see that the Italians had kept their sense of priority. Then, an hour ago, he'd begun work on the Chancellor's next Budget, drafting his initial thoughts on the pros and cons of raising National Income Tax. He is in favour but knows he will be in the minority.

He checks again that he has Holmes' and Curzon's letters of support in his pocket as well as the internal Memorandum of Approval from Robert Chalmers, his Treasury boss. Maynard has already written to Law setting out his Degas plan and has included a synopsis of these letters but he'd brought copies along, in case of need. He looks out of the window at the Downing Street bustle, not recognising any of the concerned-looking Government functionaries. But perhaps he is too distracted to register their faces properly. He frets and glances at his pocket watch. It is three-fifteen and Law is now very late for their meeting.

As he begins to read portents of gloom into the delay, Law's two secretaries, Davidson and Baldwin appear and, without speaking, gesture to him to follow. As they walk deeper into the building, noisy doors open and close on each side of the corridor as men and women hurry between offices. Whilst he had little regard for Lloyd George, since he took over as Prime Minister and with Law as his Chancellor, the atmosphere here is markedly different to the amateurish shambles of before and things are now assuredly more to Maynard's liking. From his Math background and study of Probability Theory and Applied Economics, Maynard knows the value of reliable data and his advice to Law was, from the outset, rooted in what the statistics were showing – what the evidence was telling him. Maynard's views utilised facts, not ideology or dogma, and when the facts changed so did his opinions and advice.

As Law was now one of the PM's five-person War Cabinet, Maynard's statistician's *modus operandi* was quickly seen as advantageous and embraced by the inner-circle of Government. LG ordered the building of a series of temporary huts in the gardens near Downing Street to house small teams of researchers to support this innovative system. Named the 'Garden Suburbs' by the old-school Whitehall civil servants who had become by-passed by this new breed of fact-finders, these sheds became the premises of the back-up teams to the Secretariat who took strategic decisions on industry, food and armaments production, foreign policy and trade. Lloyd George had something Asquith, his predecessor, never had; current, reliable numbers. Maynard wonders how many of the bustling bodies who now dashed past him were on their way to or from these new hot-houses of studiousness.

Davidson and Baldwin walk in front of him and stay deep in conversation until they arrive at what he knows to be the Sir John Soames dining room. Davidson turns the knob, pushes open the door and takes two paces to his left to switch on the lights. He carefully surveys the empty room to ensure that nothing 'sensitive' has been left lying around and then and only then, signals to their visitor to step inside.

"The Chancellor will be along directly. Are you well, Maynard?" he asks. Maynard smiles, nodding in affirmation without replying, distracted by the thought that Law might be about to rebuke him for concocting such an impudent, disruptive scheme which proposes expending public money on art in the middle of a World War. Why else would the Chancellor of the Exchequer wish to speak to a senior Civil Servant alone?

After Davidson leaves, Maynard gazes around. He had been in here before, of course, at lunches and dinners for visiting diplomats, but never for the discussion of internal affairs. It isn't large, about the same dimensions as a dining room in a medium-sized country house. The design, décor and furnishings however, speak of more than mere wealth. The oak panelled sidewalls are illuminated by two, specially installed skylights and the cream and gold ceiling is decorated with Greek style mouldings with horns of plenty motifs and globes in its four corners. Fine oil paintings of Kings, Queens and Statesmen hang in rich gilt frames. It is all intended to leave the occupants of the armchairs which sit around the Maplewood dining table in no doubt that they were in a place of power. Maynard has begun to idly reimagine some of the history-changing matters discussed in this room since its re-design in the 1820s when the door opens and in strides Bonar Law, a briskly moving, thick-set moustached sixty year-old, dressed formally in a grey morning suit.

"Sorry to keep you waiting, Maynard," says Law in his curious Canadian-tinged Scots accent as he sits down "…and apologies about the room. It was the only one available." He retrieves a thin file from the wedge of folders under his arm, places it carefully on the table then gestures to his Head of External Finance to be seated, "Please…"

Maynard gives him a nervous look and sits down as instructed.

The quick-witted Law had impressed him from the start, showing he was able to process, retain and then explain to others, even the most complex of economic briefings which Maynard provided. He'd also marvelled at Law's resilience when, just last year, he'd lost not one son in the war but two – Charles, killed by the Turks in Gaza, and James, shot down in his aeroplane near Arras in France. Law had returned to Government after a short break, seemingly determined to work his way through the heart-break. Though he knew neither boy well, Maynard had been deeply moved by this double tragedy, in particular by the tribute published in *The Times* to Charlie, the younger of the two. He could still recall it, word-for-word.

"Those who were privileged with the friendship of Charles Law have suffered by his death a loss which to them will not, and to his family cannot, be repaired. He was modest, affectionate, and full of the joy of life. His death marks the breaking of yet another lamp which, having shone so brightly over the home, was surely destined to shed its radiance far afield."

Charlie Law was twenty years old.

Law had lost his wife, Annie, the mother of his six children, just a few years earlier and Maynard had wondered if, in some future time, this stoic man's grief and his brave suppression of it, would be made manifest in some illness or debilitating psychology. He knows that seismic shock causes a

69

stressing of structures which sooner or later reveals itself in wide cracks or sudden, catastrophic failure. But Maynard has seen no sign of such defects yet. Not yet.

Law is at heart a staunch Conservative businessman with little affinity or time for aesthetes or abstract ideas but neither does he hold any brief for vested interest or tradition - of the City, Army, Church or Upper Classes. He is no-nonsense and practical, respecting and admiring of any plan or idea, whatever its origin, which might solve a problem or achieve progress. But now, as he dons his spectacles and thumbs his way back through his notes on Maynard's madcap Degas scheme, he frowns.

"I know that twenty-thousand pounds is small beer when the British national budget last year was six-hundred million, but I was minded to say 'no' to you on this," says Law, flicking through the last of the pages. Even upside down, Maynard recognises the letters from Holmes, Curzon and his other supporters – the contents of which he himself of course had masterminded.

"Public money on oil paintings in the middle of a war? The whole enterprise is lunacy…" continues Law, but now with an odd, wry smile playing on his lips, "…an ill-judged crusade to save the playthings of the idle rich from destruction by Philistines, an enterprise, what's more, planned by a group of fey, over-privileged intellectuals."

Maynard raises an eyebrow but says nothing. He senses that Law is provoking him for his own amusement.

"And I see that along with the other insiders you have recruited, you managed to get old Meiklejohn on your side. Did you think he would block you otherwise?"

Maynard stays silent, waiting for the rest of the scene to play out.

"You've anticipated every problem and counter-move and planned your attack accordingly. And with the auction due to start next Tuesday, none of your supporters has had time to think better of it."

Law pauses, then smiles at his so-called 'Civil Servant', giving him a look which says he isn't sure who is serving whom here.

"You'd make one hell of a chess player, Maynard."

"I prefer Bridge, Chancellor, there's more money in it."

"I'm damn pleased you're on my side and not on one of my parliamentary opponents'," says Law. Then, with no explanation, he picks out a letter from the file and begins to read it aloud. It is Maynards' own missive to Roderick Meiklejohn, the Assistant Secretary to the Treasury, sent just two days ago.

'Dear Roddy, I believe that the finance of this purchase could be arranged without throwing at this Department any immediate cash burden. Under our agreements with the French Treasury we are entitled to set off British Government expenditure in France against our loans to them. That is to say, we shall not pay out any additional cash but would get the pictures instead of getting French Government Treasury bills. The actual procedure would be an official letter to M. Avenol asking him to place the franc equivalent of £20,000 to the credit of our Embassy Account in Paris. Yours, JMK. '

"That was very well done," says Law, still looking at the note but now nodding in open admiration. "Any money we send, loan or spend in France helps their balance of payments and rather than them giving us IOUs which they'll never honour, we get the paintings instead. You can justify your gambit and there's little risk of embarrassment in Parliament."

Maynard moves uncomfortably in his seat, feeling like a conjurer whose audience has just seen his sleight of hand.

"As Meiklejohn is now one of your staunchest allies, I know he won't mind if I read out his memo back to me…"

Maynard opens his mouth to raise polite objection but Law blocks him with the raised open palm of his left hand and begins to recite the note anyway.

'Dear Chancellor, If adverse criticism arose against the proposed purchase on the ground that money should not be spent in war time, the answer is, Mr Keynes tells me, that French indebtedness to this country is on so colossal a scale that there is no prospect even within the quite distant future of Great Britain being repaid its loans. There is even some doubt whether we shall be paid interest on these loans within the near future. If therefore we spend £20,000 on the pictures, we shall be getting for our money, fine specimens of Old Masters (the non-representation of whose work in our National Gallery has long been a reproach), instead of French Treasury bills, the interest on which may quite likely not be paid.'

72

Law puts the letter back down on the table and, almost like a fellow conspirator, gives Maynard a nod of approval.

"And as Curzon, Holmes and Chalmers are all in agreement, who am I to spoil the party. I'll brief the PM then set the wheels in motion."

"Thank you, Chancellor."

Maynard can hardly believe his luck and has a wide smile on his face.

"I like to keep my troops chipper if I can," says Law. "A happy workplace is an efficient one. Besides, it'll be fun to see if you really can pull this off without getting yourself and your art shot full of holes!"

Bonar Law chortles to himself and coughs as he tidied up his papers, places them back in the file and stands up. Maynard smiles back politely. For the life of him, he can't see what there is to laugh about.

"There are just two caveats," says Law, his manner and expression returning to the serious. "You must take Austen Chamberlain with you, to the auction I mean. He'll sign the cheques and will have final say on what's purchased."

Now Maynard looks concerned.

"Don't worry, I'm sure he'll listen to Holmes' good counsel on the merits or otherwise of the paintings," says Law.

Maynard shrugs his ascent, unsure of how this will work out. They would just have to trust to Chamberlain's good sense in knowing his own limitations. Then, as he walks towards the dining room's double doors, Law delivers his second condition. It is an altogether more personal one.

"And don't do anything to put yourself, the members of the International Finance Mission or the art at risk. There must be no late night escapades, no adventures of a private nature."

His meaning is clear and Maynard returns an acknowledging tilt of the head.

"We both know what can happen when one strays-off the beaten track in strange lands," says Law, leaving no room for doubt. "Paris is full of danger now."

Maynard looks down, his eyes fixed on the floor.

"As always, there'll be an armed escort so the party will be safe – as safe as anyone can be on the edge of a battlefield. And I'll arrange for some extra measures to be put in place."

"Extra Measures? Nothing that will draw more attention to us I hope, Chancellor?"

"Just a couple of our Intelligence Service people from MI 1C; Smith-Cumming's lot, or perhaps from Captain Kell. It'll be up to them to decide which department the agents come from. They won't introduce themselves but they'll be there alright. So will their German spy counterparts I'll be bound."

"I've already warned Holmes about that. He's to disguise himself from both the Hun and the other buyers, particularly those from The Louvre. We're not sure which of them is the greatest threat," says Maynard with a grin.

"The Germans are," replies Law, humourlessly. "They'll kill you if they can."

When he returns to his office, Maynard telegrams Duncan at Charleston with a brief, triumphant message which reads "money secured for pictures."

On Saturday morning, the day before he is due to leave for France, in a telegram sent from the Post Office on the Euston Road, he follows up with more detail, this time to Nessa.

My picture coup was a whirlwind affair, carried through in a day and a half before anyone had time to reflect what they were doing. I have secured 550,000 Francs, around £20,000, to play with. Bonar Law was much amused by my wanting to buy pictures and eventually let me have my way as a sort of joke.

Holmes is travelling out with us and I hope we shall be able to attend the sale together. The prime object is to buy Ingres; his portrait of himself being first choice; after that the Perroneau. I think Holmes also has his eye on a Greco but admits there would be another chance for this. I am fairly sure I can persuade him to go for the Delacroix 'Schwiter'; I shall try very hard on the journey out to persuade him to buy a Cezanne as a personal reward to me for having got him the money, but I think his present intention is not to buy a Cezanne; I have not yet discussed the question of the Corot with him."

Vanessa replies: "We have great hopes for you and consider that your existence at The Treasury is at last justified."

Bunny Garnett had added a short note of his own: "You have been given complete absolution and future crimes also forgiven."

Maynard smiles at the reading of it.

8

À travers la Manche

Staff Train at Charing Cross Station, 1918, Alfred Hayward.

On the morning of Sunday the 24th March, Maynard and Holmes meet up with the rest of the International Financial Mission, the Inter-Ally Council as they are commonly known, at eight a.m. at Charing Cross station and are carried at speed to the south coast in their own special, Government-requisitioned train.

They stand on Folkestone Harbour's Arm Pier, waiting to board the one hundred foot long, steel-hulled packet steamer, *SS Onward,* resplendent in its dazzle-paint, bound for Boulogne and as the last of the luggage is transferred to the waiting ship, the two of them linger in the makeshift *Mole Café* talking to the Jeffrey sisters, Florence and Margaret, who with the Red Cross had provided a free buffet here for the troops since the early days of the war. The ladies are dressed in high-waisted skirts and, even on that chill spring morning, in white blouses and straw hats. Of the two, Florence is the taller and more imposing.

The building they occupy is no more than a crude, single storey lean-to, propped against the high part of the pier wall. Inside are a dozen trestle tables, a scrubbed timber serving counter and a display table with flowers and a visitor's book. On the wall are the flags of the allied nations and, strangely, with no note of explanation, an aircraft propeller. Maynard has made this journey many times before and knows the sisters well. Holmes, however, does not and after the introductions are made, Florence regales their new guest with the facts and figures she deems essential to ensure that maximum interest and educational value are derived from every visit.

"So Mister Holmes, did you know that Folkestone Harbour has seen more than ten-thousand military ships and seven thousand trains arrive and depart since the war began? Eight million passengers have come through and one-hundred and twenty thousand refugees, many from Belgium. Over thirty-nine thousand people have signed our visitor books – we have over three thousand pages of them at home!"

"Really?" Holmes replies, "That is most staggering."

Riveting though these facts are, the ladies have saved the best until last.

"And in 1915, Margaretha Geertruida Zelle…" says Florence, pausing, tilting her head to one side in a quizzical manner as if waiting for Holmes to complete her sentence.

"Mata Hari," adds Maynard, leaning towards his confused-looking friend.

"Quite so," she continues. "…the scheming trollop was stopped from boarding a ship to the continent on this very pier by Monsieur Captain Dillon of the French Secret Intelligence Service."

"And what was she like?" asks Holmes, now, for the first time, appearing to be genuinely interested.

"I'm afraid we weren't here that day…" says Margaret.

The ladies smile politely then, without further exchange, return to their duties. Maynard and Holmes pick up their mugs of tea and sit down.

"So many thousands of Belgians here in England?" says Holmes. "I had no idea."

"We think they may number a quarter of a million now. The first wave came after the civilian deaths in Leuven in August 1914, the savagery of the attack on the city shocked the world. Its library was burned to the ground and ancient pamphlet-books, the *incunables*, lost. I remember the war correspondent of the New York Tribune describing many organised civilian murders being carried out by rampaging German troops acting like 'men after an orgy'."

Maynard notices that Holmes is tightly gripping the handle of his teacup as he listens.

"The Belgians were welcomed at first of course, housed by ordinary families in and around the ports of entry and seen as plucky victims of German barbarism. But then, as the war continued and our people themselves began to suffer, their hospitality cooled somewhat," continues Maynard. "The new arrivals were returned to the places from which they had been collected and camps were built for them."

"For them to languish in poor conditions I presume?"

"No, the very opposite. Purpose-built houses of good quality, run as sovereign colonies under Belgian governance. But even this caused resentment – they had running water and electric lighting whilst many of their British neighbours did not."

"An understandable if not very Christian response."

"Particularly as our casualty lists grew longer and the hardships deeper. Adversity brings out the worst in us as well as the best," says Maynard, ruefully. "And when the war is over, our guests will quickly be shown the door and their presence here swiftly forgotten. The British have never been keen on foreigners, even less so on immigrants in large numbers."

"And yet most Britons are themselves the descendants of migrants."

"Who have then pulled up the drawbridge. It has, sadly, been ever thus."

Just as Maynard finishes speaking, they are called by the sound of the ship's foghorn signalling its readiness to depart and so give the sisters their thanks and bid farewell. Outside, Holmes finds himself offering up a silent prayer for his own safe return and quickly feels the guilt of his fear. He beats it back into its cage, takes a final deep breath on home soil then walks up the *Onward's* gangway. The two friends join the rest of their party on the First Class sundeck and just before noon, the mooring lines are released and the ship moves away from the pier, out into the deep water. As Holmes says his goodbyes to England, he wonders if he will ever see her again.

For Maynard, standing looking out across the Channel, the omens are good. The clouds have been blown away and a gentle breeze should mean their journey across the flat sea will feel more like a pleasure cruise than a Mad Hatter mission into wartime danger. A hundred yards from the shore, Maynard turns and looks back at Folkestone town as it lays nestled against the backdrop of the South Downs, the white chalk-faced sea cliffs running away north-eastwards towards Dover. To the west, the coast curves gently in a twenty mile arc taking in Hythe, Dymchurch and Romney Marshes before ending at the far-off shingle foreland at flat Dungeness. Maynard says his own fond goodbyes but fancies he can already taste the success of a triumphant homecoming.

The others in their party seem relaxed enough as they lean against the ship's rail in the sunshine. The Inter-Ally Council comprises the Lord Buckmaster and Sir Alfred Booth, both with their male secretaries. Austen Chamberlain of course is there alongside Geoffrey Storrs Fry, an administrator from the Treasury, the six-foot four-inch American lawyer Paul Cravath, representing the USA and General Mola, who would speak for Italy. Maynard will serve the other allies although, as he had explained to Holmes on the train journey down, he suspects that Belgium, Serbia and Armenia would have already made representations to their hosts, the French, in order that their interests were duly protected. The Treasury's own functionary, Mr Berry, is there to ensure that all material needs were met and on the decks below, a small group of clerks and servants as well as a dozen armed soldiers remain on constant stand-by. As they'd boarded the *Onward*, Maynard had also noticed the presence of a uniformed medical doctor and two nurses; one a sturdy male, the other an open-faced, sinewy young woman. How familiar her almond-shaped eyes had seemed to him. Looking down on them now from his position on the sundeck, he can see that the three medics stand apart from the rest of the group but speak little to each other. In the few minutes he observes them, he notes that when they do converse, it is the smiling female nurse who seems to hold sway - the body language of her male companions showing just a modicum of deference although she is of lower military rank.

The *Onward* is barely ten minutes out from Folkestone when two gunmetal-grey warships appear on the western horizon and cruising at great speed, quickly gain on them before becoming protective bookending companions; one astern, the other two hundred yards ahead off the starboard bow. No sooner have the destroyers taken up their convoy positions than a dark speck in the sky grows to become a huge silver Zeppelin-like airship hovering above them, the insignia of the Royal Flying Corps emblazoned on its tail section.

This *SS Class* inflatable bomb-shaped monster is fifty yards long and thirty at least in diameter and everyone on deck stares up at this miracle of modern technology, wide-eyed and open-mouthed. Few on board would have ever seen such a weapon this close before. It has an improvised gondola – a stripped-back wingless, rudderless, propellered plane fuselage hanging down beneath its belly carrying its two pilots, and a powerful engine which whirrs loudly and occasionally splutters in the morning air. In Maynard's mind, the reassurance that they were being given such an escort quickly turns to disquiet. This protection is there to spot and destroy mines, submarines and enemy ships - two of His Majesty's destroyers and an airship were with them because they needed to be, to save a ship of international dignitaries from destruction. He glances across at Holmes but after noticing his earlier apprehension he now sees nothing but wonder and decides to leave it that way. There is time enough for rational fear to take root in his companion's mind.

Even though the weather is fine, the spring air is chill and after an hour the two men retreat to the lounge and settle into velvet-covered armchairs before ordering hot, sweet tea.

"And what were your wife's thoughts when you told her of our little excursion?" asks Maynard.

"For some reason, she assumed that because I agreed to do it and that we are guarded, it is both necessary and quite safe."

Maynard raises an eyebrow as if to say 'perhaps you should have told just a little more of the risks involved'.

"She came to Charing Cross this morning to see me off."

"How very nice," says Maynard, for a moment reflecting that he had no such supporter to bid him Godspeed.

"And how go her musical endeavours?"

"They progress well, thank you."

"Ah, music – the human soul speaking without words."

"Yes, quite. She is teaching of course and has had several recitals of late..."

"I have been meaning to re-examine Pythagorean theory, you know, all that music of the spheres stuff, heavenly bodies ringing out measurable vibrations based on their orbits and distances from each other. Fascinating."

Holmes frowns at the interruption but then smiles, humouring his friend. He fears there will be much of this before they return home to London.

"She did consider coming to Paris with us - the Boulanger sisters are somewhere on the outskirts and she wished to meet them," says Holmes. "I think she half-supposed that Nadia or Lili could have been persuaded to write her a piece for violin."

"I doubt we will have time to see them but I can enquire?"

"Dear Maynard," says Holmes, affectionately, "…always so ready to broker social and professional connections. But I fear this time there will be insufficient hours in the day."

"And I have heard that composer Ethel Smyth is near Paris too. She has been volunteering, working as a radiologist, since 1915."

"I thought she was a pacifist, against even the suffragettes' support of the war?"

"She was but then like so many, reconsidered – felt she must do something to help."

Holmes frowns and looks away.

"I wonder if some of the criticism she received played a part in her going?" Maynard adds.

Holmes says nothing, not even acknowledging the arrival of the cups of steaming beverage, delivered by a girl in a neat pinafore dress.

"She has the requisite technical abilities but if she writes with power and vitality, the critics say that she lacks feminine charm," says Maynard. "Then when she writes with delicacy they say she lacks strength of her male counterparts. It is nothing more than brazen misogyny – and they doubtless disapprove too of her love of other women. But she is one of our best, Beecham says so and he does not bestow his approval whimsically."

"And now she works on the wards?" Holmes asks.

"At the French military hospital at Vichy."

"So she's treating the wounded and the dying, putting herself in the harm's way of infection, hunger and German guns?"

Maynard nods.

"And Vaughan Williams too faces the reaper daily," he adds. "He volunteered at the outbreak of war at the age of forty-two! He's been driving ambulances through mud, shit and shellfire and I hear he's now in the artillery, somewhere in France."

"And that after he lost George Butterworth in '16," says Holmes ruefully, more to himself than to his friend. "He'd been helping Ralph reconstruct his first symphony after the first draft was lost. George was killed in the Somme battle, somewhere near **Pozières**, north-east of Amiens. I looked it up before we left. Our train will be passing quite close by…" he says, his words trailing off as he remembers again the reports of the young composer's death. A sniper's bullet to the head, a body quickly buried in the side of a trench, the relentless bombardments meaning the body was never recovered for his family to grieve over at a Christian burial.

"...are we not ashamed that we have hidden from duty so long in such sheltered comfort?"

Maynard is about to take a sip of tea but seeing the look on Holmes' face, stops mid-movement and puts his cup down. His friend has suddenly descended into morbid distress.

"I do *what* I can, given *who* I am, as do you," says Maynard, quietly. "My friends would have me withdraw from our present peril, cease serving the nation at our Treasury. Some of them call me 'the war mongers' accountant'. It pains me deeply but each of us is answerable only to our own conscience. You are the best, most able safe-keeper of our country's greatest art treasures and must fulfil *that* duty."

"The French have a word for men like me," replies Holmes, unconvinced.

"The French have a word for everything!" continues Maynard, trying to lighten the mood but to no good effect.

"They would call me *embusque*. It means shirker - someone who avoids military service by obtaining a government job."

"I know what it means."

Maynard is about to say more when they are joined by Austen Chamberlain. Maynard darts a glance at Holmes as if to say 'we'll continue this later,' then they stand up to shake the new arrival's hand. They'd been in different compartments on the train down from London and this is their first meeting of the day.

A fluent speaker of European languages and lately the Secretary of State for India, Chamberlain had been the perfect choice for Chairman of the Inter-Ally Council. Knowledgeable on international matters, a hitherto alarmed observer of the growth of German Nationalism, a principled politician and good public servant; he and Maynard had always got along well even though others thought Austen's manner stiff and from a bygone age. Such a reputation bothers him not one jot. His monocle and frock-coated elegance reinforce the Victorian theatrical effect and he oozes the poise and refinement of the well-heeled and the well-bred. As if modelling himself on his father, Joseph, he is determinedly 'un-modern.'

"Mr Cravath wishes to discuss interest payments with you," says Chamberlain leaning towards Maynard conspiratorially, before sipping his cup of hot chocolate. "I believe he's well-disposed towards you. This might be an opportune moment to find out what he wants and set out our stall before the minuted business gets underway in Paris?"

"I know what he *says* he wants," replies Maynard in a suitably hushed tone. "To lend us money at seemingly advantageous interest rates and help us win the war. What he *really* wants is for all the gold in the world to reside in America in exchange for giving paper money to Europe at interest rates which are advantageous only to themselves." Maynard smirks a little. Like a market haggler, he knows he has the measure of his adversary.

"The war has provided them with much of the economic oxygen we are now increasingly short of," continues Maynard, now turning to explain the situation to Holmes. "We are *in extremis* and they know it. We may have to give in to them."

"One might almost think they encouraged the war to happen!" says Holmes, delivering his conspiracy theory with an ironic chuckle.

Chamberlain says nothing, glancing quickly around the room to check for eavesdroppers before raising an eyebrow in Maynard's' direction. Both men shake their heads and frown at Holmes, signalling to him to keep his quips to himself. The Inter-Ally meeting in Paris will be a difficult enough confluence, soured by feelings of suspicion and distrust without accusations of disingenuousness being openly flung around.

"Why don't we talk through our plans for the auction …quietly," says Maynard.

9

Intermède à Boulogne sur Mer

The Hotel Christol, Boulogne. 1918, Ernest Proctor.

It is just after two p.m., with the port of Boulogne in sight, when the *Onward*'s deck hands busy themselves with preparations for arrival and the airship and destroyer guardians peel-away home, mission accomplished.

Twenty minutes later, as they tie-up at the main pier, the realities of being in a country at war become apparent. They find themselves moored behind a ship being uploaded with the last of its cargo of battle-weary soldiers, heading home. Many walk slowly as if carrying an imagined burden. At its rear, along a dedicated gangway away from the still able-bodied, a line of infirm and blinded troops are led by nurses as they shuffle forward. It is a tragic sight. But there is worse. Amongst them are those on stretchers, laying quite motionless, asleep or drugged by pain-killing opiates. Some of course, Maynard knows, will not survive the crossing to see the White Cliffs of home. The ship's funnels belch the black smoke of imminent departure, whistles blow and men shout, urging-on the collective effort to get the vessel launched as soon as possible. Tethered there, helpless and unprotected, they are sitting ducks for the bombs of German planes.

Out on the harbour's now choppy waters, hearty tugs, cabin cruisers, schooners, brigantines, barques and barges – even Royal Navy sea planes, bustle and bob around. On the quaysides and service roads, soldiers, uniformed officials and dock workers, move about the place in a state of perturbed nervousness as if every day spent here, just doing a simple job of work, could be their last.

Maynard and Holmes stand in the afternoon sun considering what to do next. They look towards the buildings along the seafront which before the war would have been a well-kept, elegant terrace. Now, the stuccoed frontages are tired and stained; their interiors press-ganged into war service to become telegraph offices, command centres and storerooms. Above their grey roofs, the houses of the old town can be seen marching up steep slopes towards the city's medieval castle, the domed cathedral of its *Sacre-*

Coure and the remains of a large windmill. Beyond, to the south-west, the fields of northern France can just be made out in the far distance.

It is to the Hotel Christol, located in one of the quayside buildings, that the Englishmen decide to adjourn as the luggage is unloaded from the ship and taken to the waiting Paris train in the harbour's own dedicated railway terminus. It will leave in one hour but is not due to arrive in the capital until early the next morning and the two friends agree that a good meal is needed. They do not know when they might eat well again.

The Christol had been commandeered at the beginning of the war by the Red Cross and used as a hostel and restaurant for those of their workers passing through Boulogne. Somehow Maynard manages to not only wangle a table but secures one next to the window looking out on the harbour. After they have ordered a plentiful buffet, he begins to explain the workings of the 'dazzle' paint now used on the superstructure of allied ships to an already disinterested-looking Holmes.

"Being an artist, I believe you'll find this most riveting," he begins.

Holmes smiles politely and puts a piece of baguette into his mouth. He prays that this lecture, he cannot remember if it is the second or third of the day, will not take too long.

"In order for a U-boat to successfully torpedo a ship, it has to predict the speed and direction of its target and then aim in front of it."

Holmes' heart sinks. This diatribe will almost certainly give him indigestion.

"And it only has thirty seconds before the wake of the periscope is spotted and the U-boat's position given away. This all happens between 350 yards and 1 mile distance to give the torpedo time to arm itself once unleashed. The subs carry only twelve 'eels of death' and so they have to get it right first time."

Holmes looks blankly back at Maynard, continuing to munch on his bread.

"Unfortunately, they did get it right and caused carnage. Then, last autumn, the Merchant Naval Service came up with the idea of 'dazzling' rather than camouflaging. They paint swathes and stripes of contrasting colours onto the sides of the hull and funnels to obscure its shape, size and direction…curves creating a false bow wave, angled stripes on the funnel making it look like it's facing in the opposite direction…that sort of thing."

"A series of optical illusions," says Holmes, beginning to mildly warm to the topic.

"Exactly."

"Thank God the *SS Onward* has been so attired."

"It has, but the effect only works when the target is viewed via a periscope. It is no defence against German mines, airships, aeroplanes or ships."

"But at least it protects us from the submarines," says Holmes, "I would've hated being torpedoed. Shells, mines or bombs are far more preferable."

Maynard laughs and drops the subject. As the bisque soup, sausage-filled rolls and duck pâté arrive on the table he launches into another topic he believes will be of greater interest to his companion.

"They're converting the Casino here," he says, gesturing towards the southern end of the harbour. "It was the old Palais de Neptune but now it will be a military hospital. Roulette wheels and *Chemin de fer* tables replaced by operating theatres, beds and laboratories! An American, a Doctor Cushing, is to work there. He sounds like a marvellous chap with fantastical ideas about using electromagnets to remove shrapnel from the brains of our injured boys. He has raised a question mark over our Government's resourcing though – thinks we won't put in enough doctors, nurses, stretcher bearers and the rest; that we can't manage the place properly. I dare say he'll be proved right."

"Can't you do anything?" asks Holmes.

"Shouldn't think so," Maynard says, pessimistically. "The problems of any state-run system can be traced to its national values and because our free-market economy holds sway, good health is just another chargeable commodity. We cannot roll out large scale medical provision because the structures simply don't exist. This will not change until there is free treatment for all."

"That will never happen!" says Holmes incredulously.

"It could be paid for by a country-wide insurance scheme. All would pay-in according to income but would receive the same good treatment regardless of monetary status."

Maynard winks at his sceptical friend as if to say, 'it's going to happen one day, I'm going to see to it'. Then he glances at his watch.

"Holy hellfire! We have to go – the train departs in ten minutes."

Holmes is still eating when Maynard stands up, dons his overcoat and hurries across to the cashier to pay the bill. He has forgotten to bring French francs with him and so hands over double the cost of the meal in English pounds. But the *Maître De* seems pleased with the transaction and gives his now rushing guests a warm *au revoir* and *bon chance*.

On their trot back towards the train, they are obliged to stop to allow several platoons of newly disembarked troops to pass. They are chipper young fellows, marching in time to their own small fife and drum band. The tune is a well-known one and under his breath, Holmes lightly joins in.

Some talk of Alexander, and some of Hercules
Of Hector and Lysander, and such great names as these.
But of all the world's brave heroes, there's none that can compare.
With a tow, row, row, to the British Grenadiers.

As the last of the soldiers march clear and their anthem fades in the direction of the waiting lorries at the end of the quayside road, Holmes looks at Maynard.

"Now we go into a small battle of our own and like it or not, you are our Lysander."

Maynard nods at Holmes with a half-smile but says nothing more as they resume their hurried walk. Yes, they would need courage but he will not equate their mission to those who had just passed by on a journey to hell.

They make the train by the skin of their teeth and Maynard, heart beating and pulse racing, is obliged to pull down the window of their compartment to take in much-needed oxygen. As the train whistle blows and they pull out of the harbour station, he sees a tall, moustachioed man in a train guard's uniform walk quickly from behind a stanchion to jump on to the open footplate at the rear of the train's baggage car. Maynard doesn't think too much about it until, looking back down the lines of carriages, he sees that the female nurse in their party has been watching the late-boarder. She waits for a few seconds to see if the man remains on the train and when he does, she disappears back inside and closes her window.

The train moves slowly through Boulogne's harbour town and shabby suburbs, following the River Liane inland for about three miles before turning south to run parallel to the coast. Maynard knows that progress to Paris will be slow as the driver would keep their speed down so as to monitor the condition of the tracks. Stoppages will be frequent to be sure that the way ahead is safe from bombardment and marauding bands of

German troops. They are due in the capital tomorrow morning. That will be Monday the 25th March. The Degas auction is the following day.

The two friends settle in their compartment and as the train ambles lazily through the sunny afternoon, it is hard to believe they are on the edge of an actual war. They pass the occasional shattered house or burnt hillside but these signs aside, they could be in peacetime Hauts-de-France on some pleasant journey south. They read, chat, drink tea and nap. Maynard intermittently wanders up and down the train and spends time with other members of the Inter-Ally Council, talking shop. But in the evening, around eight o'clock, as they cross the River Somme near the hamlet of Colline-Beaumont, things begin to change. Across the fields, to the east, the first sounds of artillery can be heard. It begins as a series of distant staccato bangs, perhaps three or four every minute, which become louder and more frequent and by the time they are readying themselves for a night in their couchettes, as they approach the town of Abbeville, the flash of canon lights-up the horizon, the exploding shells are throaty booms which vibrate the ground beneath them. There is no doubt now that they are very near to a battlefield, close to the Western Front of *le Grande Guerre* – a land of craters, fox holes, trenches and black skeletal trees.

Thirty miles further on, at two a.m., in Amiens, the train stops and there it stays, stuck in the middle of a bombing raid on the town. The two men lie awake, neither speaking, awaiting fate's ruling. Even under the bed linen in his berth, Maynard is fully dressed right down to his brown brogues and has kept his Treasury briefcase close at hand. In the darkness, he distracts himself from the thought that one of the metal casings full of high explosives may have his name scrawled upon it in *Deutsch Gothic* font by remembering, word for word, every letter he'd ever written to Duncan. Then he runs through the loan-to-repayment calculations he will need for the upcoming negotiations with the Americans. When he finishes, he goes back through the entire silent recitation all over again.

In the bed below, wearing only his *Porosknit* combination woollen underwear, Holmes surprises himself. Back in London, at home or in his office, when the Zeppelins were in the air above and the bombs were falling, he had found himself in a state of helpless, withering fear. Now, perhaps because he has knowingly put himself in harm's way to do his nation's duty, feeble though it is compared to the efforts of other men, he is resigned to whatever might come. No longer impotent bystander, he is now a proud participant and even when a shell lands just yards away, causing the carriage to lurch violently sideways, he lays steady and emboldened. His only thought is that if the worst happens, he will make a good fist of it, be master of own his terror so as not to distress the witnesses of his passing.

When, after two hours, the explosions finally cease, a song begins to run through his mind, ferrying him gently towards much-needed sleep. The sweet melody of *'To Gratiana Dancing and Singing'* had been written by William Denis 'Billy' Browne, killed in 1915 at Gallipoli, to the words of Richard Lovelace, a cavalier poet. It has come to him quite unaccountably.

He remembers that his wife had sung it to him last weekend at home in Hampstead, as she sat at the piano.

So did she move; so did she sing
Like the harmonious spheres that bring
Unto their rounds their music's aid;
Which she performed such a way,
As all th' enamoured world will say:
The Graces danced, and Apollo play'd.

As the last notes die away, a single tear runs down his cheek.

Maynard remains awake, still combating his present jeopardy with thoughts of Duncan Grant. He wishes, in a moment of spiritual weakness for which he swiftly reproaches himself that he was now abed in Charleston, safe in the maternal folds of Sussex's sweet Downlands.

10

Grave Warnings

Villa Belle Vue After Air Raid, 1918. Adrian Hill.

They awake at 6.30 the next morning to find the train has made steady, if slow progress towards Paris. Geoffrey Fry joins them for a meagre breakfast of black coffee, hard croissant and stale cracked cheese in what passes for a buffet car. Mr. Berry tries to ease their hunger by distributing fresh apples and dates but as soon as he is out of earshot, the affable Fry leans across the table to quietly pass on some alarming news.

"The Germans are shelling Paris," he says under his breath. "The captain of our troopers has just told me – although their artillery is still sixty miles away from the city, there are explosions near the *Sacre Coeur.*"

"Surely that's not possible?" says an incredulous Holmes.

"We think they may have a new gun," whispers Maynard, now sharing a secret slice of intelligence. "We've known they had something terrible for the past month but it would hardly have helped national morale for it to be common knowledge. If this story is true, it is a most unpleasant confirmation."

"I have heard it said that technologies advance exponentially in wartime," mutters Holmes, still shaking his head in disbelief. "I suppose one could say that when the war is finally over, at least some material progress will have come from it."

"The development of more efficient ways to kill each other you mean. How very wonderful," says Maynard.

Fry too looks disapproving. Holmes reminds himself that though a senior secretary at the Treasury and part of the war effort, Fry has been raised as a Quaker, part of the Fry's cocoa family in Bristol. Quakers, the Society of Friends, holds that war is contrary to Christian teachings, that we must love our brothers and sisters, not do them harm. In the second Boer War, during three years of scorched earth policies against the white South

African farmer population, of concentration camps and diseased, starving children, Quakers protested with dignified vigour and were in turn damned by their own countrymen. Though no Quaker himself, Holmes feels an affinity because of their worthy peace-making and for their shared belief in social reformation and Adult Education. Whilst the Fry family are not as radically pacifist as their rival Cadbury or Rowntree dynasties, others who promote chocolate as an ethical alternative to alcohol, Holmes must tread more carefully when discussing matters of war and peace.

"The bombardment began two days ago, on Saturday morning. And not from aeroplanes or Zeppelins. Scores of Parisians have been killed," Fry continues.

"Is this just rumour or verifiable fact?" asks Maynard.

"The numbers of the fatalities may be exaggerated but I believe the substance of the story to be correct. Paris is attacked."

Fry finishes his cup of cold coffee, grimacing and dabbing his mouth, when his attention is caught by Chamberlain, waving to him from the far end of the carriage.

"I'm sorry, Austen wants to speak to me. Don't worry Holmes, all will be well. The breakfasts at the Hotel Crillon are very wonderful!"

"He always seems so optimistic," says Holmes when Fry is gone. "Best foot forward and all that..."

"The British Empire was built on that same spirit."

"And yet he's had a torrid time over the past two years I hear."

"There's been death in the family and he lost Rupert Brooke in March '15. Rupert enjoyed the company of men as well as of women, of course," says Maynard, lowering his voice. "So Geoffrey married Alathea Gardner just two months later. Practical solutions to the problems of heartbreak. It is the way of the Anglo-Saxon male."

"We all put on a brave face," agrees Holmes, "but reveal our frailties eventually. I heard that Allenby who is the most resilient of men, hadn't spoken of his grief for his son killed in action, nor shown any sign of it, yet he broke down in tears when reading one of Rupert's poems at the memorial service for his darling boy."

"Yes, he was already a very great poet.

There's some corner of a foreign field

That is forever England. There shall be

In that rich earth a richer dust concealed…"

As Maynard pauses to recall the next lines, Holmes finishes the poem for him.

"*…laughter, learnt of friends; and gentleness*

In hearts at peace, under an English heaven."

The two men look at each other thoughtfully and exchange thin smiles. Rupert's lament may yet be applied to them. Holmes remembers too that

103

Brooke was a friend of Billy Browne. Neither man says anything more until they reach the outskirts of Creil, thirty miles from Paris.

As the train nears the centre of the town, Maynard sees that panic has spread amongst the inhabitants of this important railway junction. They are not seeking shelter from the shelling, he thinks – they are leaving their homes behind them, looking to escape a battle which threatens to engulf them, fleeing from an advancing army. The streets are busy with baggage-laden families, their faces taut with anxiety. Some push the wheel-chaired elderly in the direction of the station whilst others lead dogs or pull a reluctant goat. Cars, trucks and wagons can be seen tilting under the load of occupants and possessions. Houses and shops are abandoned, their windows and doors shuttered or boarded-up. Beyond the station and the River Oise, on a high hill above the town, the medieval castle of Mortefontaine stands stripped of all flags and proud standards, its stone walls an outmoded defence against twentieth-century shellfire and bombs.

When the train comes to a standstill, their soldier escort are the first to jump onto the platform, forming an armed guard on the carriage doors, bayonets at the ready. It is a prudent measure but as it turns out, needless – the hundreds of fearful refugees are waiting for trains travelling north-west, away from Paris, not towards it.

Holmes and Maynard get permission to disembark in search of a local newspaper and information on the shelling of Paris. They eventually find a newsstand but *les journaux* contain no useful news at all. In the ticket hall, as they turn the pages in vain and ask for intelligence from anyone who will listen, Maynard sees the captain of their troopers and the female nurse, hurry into the Station Master's office and close the door behind them. After ten more minutes of futile enquiry, Maynard and Holmes return to the train, none the wiser. As soon as the nurse and soldier are back on board, they set off south towards Paris and God knows what.

Twenty minutes later Maynard is summoned to a meeting of Chamberlain, Buckmaster, Booth, Geoffrey Fry and the captain of their troop escort, a Captain Crimmond. Maynard is surprised to see that the almond-eyed Staff Nurse is there too. They are ushered into the buffet car and with the compartment doors locked at both ends and soldiers standing guard outside, the briefing begins.

"We have grave tidings," says Crimmond. "In hindsight, we should never have allowed this expedition to leave England. Germany has launched a major new offensive. It began on the 21st March, three days ago."

To the men's amazement, the nurse then speaks. She doesn't introduce herself.

"The German's are calling it *Kaiserschlacht* – the Kaiser's Battle," she says. "For those of you who do not know, the background to this action is that the Americans have arrived in France and will be fully engaged in the fighting by June. The German civilian population is suffering terribly because of our blockades – food, raw materials, and, consequently, munitions, may run out at any time. They have reasoned they cannot hold on too much longer. The November peace treaty with Bolshevik Russia means their eastern armies are freed-up to be used against us and they've decided it's now or never – that this is their final and best chance to win."

Her light manner which Maynard had observed earlier has changed to one of utter seriousness. It occurs to Maynard that *this* is her real purpose here – she is a guardian agent, a sentinel; it was the sisterly nurse which was the counterfeit.

She looks around the room to make sure she has everyone's attention before continuing on. No-one even thinks of asking who she really is or by what right she is there. She has established her unchallengeable credentials.

"As far as we can tell, there are three separate but coordinated offensives. From intercepted messages we have learnt they are codenamed *Michael, Georgette* and *Blücher–Yorck*. *Georgette* will be conducted at Ypres and is intended to distract and confuse. *Blücher* is against the French in the Champagne region. *Michael* is the one which concerns us here and now, and is taking place along a forty mile front. They are throwing at least thirty-five divisions against us – that's over seven-hundred thousand men."

Amongst her audience, there is an audible intake of breath at the scale of the attack.

"From aerial reconnaissance and our interrogation of German deserters, we knew a major spring offensive was being prepared but this is more ambitious than anyone expected."

"General Ludendorff intends to advance across the Somme River," interjects Crimmond. "They will then wheel north-west to sever the British lines of communication behind the Artois front, trapping the British Expeditionary Force in Flanders. Allied forces will be drawn away from our main supply ports at Boulogne and Calais, which the Germans will then attack and overrun. Then they will take Paris. Our armies will be surrounded, cut-off and have to surrender. That's their plan anyway. It's up to us to stop them."

"And can we?" asks Geoffrey Fry, urgently.

Neither the nurse nor Crimmond answers – they only exchange nervous glances.

"For the avoidance of any doubt, we want the ungarnished truth," says a forceful Chamberlain. "What's the situation?"

"The *situation,* Mr Chamberlain, is bloody awful," the nurse tells him.

The men don't turn a hair at the use of such language by a woman for it is now obvious that she is with them; one of the chaps, part of the fight.

"The Germans have captured many prisoners and we have great losses. We are only three hundred thousand against three-quarters of a million."

"They've overrun Roye and we're being driven west," Crimmond goes on. "Their Storm Troopers took full advantage of the foggy weather to punch-through our front line and attack HQ positions and communications centres. Then they come at us from behind. The need for French reinforcements is urgent. We've lost the line of the Somme except for a stretch between the Omignon and the Tortille and the Third Army had to give ground as it tried to maintain contact with the left flank of the Fifth.

107

As of last night, France's General Pétain is concerned that the British Fifth Army is beaten and that the might of the German offensive is about to be launched against French forces in Champagne. He's reluctant to help us."

"So, gentlemen, the question is do you wish to continue on to Paris or not?" says the nurse. "Even if you complete your business before the city falls, we may not be able to get you back to England - your route home could be cut-off as the Germans sweep across the country."

Chamberlain speaks up without hesitation.

"The meeting of the Finance Mission is vital to the war effort – money is a weapon too. This present battle may not go our way but the conflict will go on and the means to pay for it must be determined. The American loans are the life blood of the fight and without them, we shall die."

"That's why we're here," says Crimmond gesturing towards the nurse and, with a vague circular wave, in the general direction of the accompanying soldiers. "The Government and the army understand your importance."

All in the room nod their approval.

"There is one other thing," says the nurse. "Some of you have heard rumours that the Germans have developed a new long-range weapon," she says, pausing just long enough for the men to brace themselves for more bad news. "I regret to tell you this is true."

A new look of concern spreads around the room.

"You've probably heard of the *Big Berthas*. They were first used back in '14, had seventeen inch shells, a range of six miles and caused much havoc. But this new canon is terror incarnate. They're calling it the *Emperor William* gun and we think its range is seventy-five miles."

For a full five seconds there is shocked silence before Chamberlain speaks, his words delivered slowly as the implications of this revelation begin to dawn on him. "My God...like being able to fire a canon from Hyde Park and have it hit Kings College Chapel in Cambridge. If they overrun the Channel ports, they'll be able to attack the Home Counties, perhaps even London itself."

"The size of the shell isn't as large as the *Berthas*, only about nine inches in diameter," says Crimmond, ignoring Chamberlain's correct but alarming realisation. "But we've learned that the barrel is 120 feet long and its shells achieve an altitude of more than 25 miles above the earth."

The whole room stares at him in amazement.

"That's five times the height of Mount Everest," says Maynard. "They've launched a projectile into space and landed it precisely on a small, pre-determined target. They would have had to calculate the *Coriolis Effect* – a navigational allowance for the rotation of the earth. It is quite unbelievable."

Crimmond frowns, momentarily non-plussed by Keynes' donning of his Applied Mathematician's hat. "The destructive power on the ground is relatively small – but its real purpose is psychological," he goes on. "When the shells hit Paris two days ago, they thought a high-altitude Zeppelin was dropping bombs on them. There was no sound or sight of the enemy, just explosions with no warning. They landed on the *Quai de la Seine*. That's only three miles from the *Place de la Concorde*, the *Champs-Elysees* and the Paris Opera House."

"It's a siege gun but the target isn't buildings or people, its morale," adds the nurse.

"The explosions could be heard right across Paris. They counted 21 shells on the first day, landing at regular intervals. Fifteen people were killed and thirty-six wounded. We hear that many hundreds are already queuing at the stations, at Gare d'Orsay and at Gare Montparnasse," says Crimmond.

"We expect thousands more will try to leave the city," says the nurse. "Fear is spreading like an epidemic..."

"We'll not be scared back into our rabbit holes by Hun gunfire, however advanced its mechanisation," proclaims Chamberlain. "I vote to press-on."

As the meeting choruses a determined *hear! hear!*, Crimmond and the nurse nod at their audience as if to say, "We thought you might say that." Then they look at each other, holding each other's gaze for a few seconds, as if steeling themselves for the difficult days ahead.

When he returns to his compartment, Maynard says nothing about the likelihood of Germans' overrunning Paris but confirms the existence of the monster gun. Holmes says only that "…at least this should ensure we'll have the auction rooms to ourselves."

Maynard looks back at him with a half-smile then turns tight lipped to stare out of the window. On the horizon, he can see the distant city, a pencil-thin line of cream-grey Lutetian limestone under gathering rain clouds.

11

Bonjour à Paris

At 11.30 a.m., their train rolls into Gare du Nord and the Inter-Ally Council disembarks to platforms full of agitated civilians but few soldiers or police. Then, as Maynard and Holmes make their way through the crowds, they are welcomed by the cries of newspaper sellers proclaiming that "*le canon n'a pas tire depuis neuf heures!*"

Maynard appears indifferent to the news that the monster gun has not fired for nine hours, being more concerned with the fate of his luggage. Holmes though reminds himself that Paris will soon be surrounded, a fortress without walls but a city under siege nevertheless. Remembrances of schoolboy history flash through his mind – ghoulish tales of starvation, disease and havoc. He must stay vigilant, be wary of others. He and Maynard will bag the Degas art then be gone as quickly as a north-bound train will carry them, two days from now.

"Debussy décède à Paris!" calls out another newsboy.

Holmes flinches, he knows how his musician wife will be saddened. Whilst many disapproved of the goings-on in the great man's not so very private life, his reputation as a composer remained unsullied. He wonders if Debussy was killed by the gun.

"At least the shelling has stopped," says Holmes, as together with Chamberlain and Maynard, he pushes his way through more flustered Parisians and emerges onto the station forecourt. "Perhaps our brave boys have bombed it back to hell?"

"If it has ceased to fire, there may be mechanical failure – the 'teething troubles,' of innovation," says Maynard, as he opens the door to a taxi cab and climbs in. "But whatever the explanation, it won't be because of a sudden German compassion for unarmed civilians. War makes devils of us all."

The Council members are to stay at the Hotel de Crillon, situated at the end of the Champs-Elysees, where their meetings will also be held. Each is to make their own way there and their luggage will be transported later. Maynard has seen their troop escort leave the train and be marshalled to attention on the platform. He assumes they will be billeted at a hostel somewhere close to the Crillon. But of the so-called medical team and the tall, moustached guard who had jumped onto the train at Boulogne, he sees nothing more.

The journey to the hotel takes less than ten minutes but whilst the station and its surrounding streets have seethed with crowded bustle, the avenues and boulevards which run south-west are empty. Shops and businesses are locked and shuttered, the curtains and blinds of townhouses and apartments, drawn across the windows of darkened rooms. It is as if the population has either left Paris or have retired to their cellars, fearful but resigned, waiting for the Germans to overrun them. There are bomb craters and shell holes in the roads and pavements, some are under crude repair, others left to fill with rain and become muddy ponds. A sense of unease settles on the three men. They sit in silence looking out at the sooty buildings under the grey Monday morning clouds. Never has Paris looked less like the City of Light. Holmes wonders if their adventure will end in an internment camp or worse.

As they pull up in front of the hotel, Maynard thinks the place looks unchanged, just as it has always been. An island in a sea of troubles. He knows it became a hotel in 1909 but that it was originally one of a pair of adjacent mansions, *Le Garde-Meuble de la Couronne*, the Department for State Furniture, and the other the Ministry of the Marine, both built by Louis XV in the 1750s to be grand offices of state for the French Government. Instead, *Le Garde-Meuble* building had been taken over by a succession of French aristocrats before being confiscated by the 1789 revolutionaries, re-appropriated for Government use and made a centre for international diplomatic meetings. The first trade agreement between the then new French Republic and the fledgling United States of America was signed here. Before the present war, visiting Heads of State would occupy its suites and meet their French hosts. Now, the allied generals use the hotel to meet, dine, drink and plan their campaigns. But it had been a palace and still looked like one.

As they walk into the foyer and sign-in at the desk, Holmes takes in the Crillon's splendour. Every surface is covered in ornament; cornices, mouldings, wall panelling, gilt-framed mirrors and paintings. Not one square inch has been left unadorned. Heavy crystal chandeliers are everywhere.

"I detest this place," mutters Maynard, "it is obscene. Such excess is morally abhorrent and the flaunting of it, provocative. Even the horses of the French aristocracy lived like kings – just look at the stables at Chantilly. No wonder they had a bloody revolution. Louis the sixteenth and his queen were guillotined right out there to make that very point," he says, gesturing towards the Place de la Concorde. "And yet the well-to-do still hold court here. The privileged wear no crowns but are a nobility nonetheless."

Holmes and Chamberlain nod their agreement but the irony of being here, about to enjoy its dubious luxury, is not lost on them. Both have reservations about Maynard's sort of politics and bridle just a little. He has again shown why, in some quarters, he is called a 'Bloomsbury Socialist'. But though he would sometimes be challenged, few, if any, could best him in political or philosophical debate. Both men know that even Maynard's own words cannot keep pace with the speed of his mind but nevertheless, Chamberlain decides to skirmish.

"You and I live well on the back of a system of privilege, do we not, Maynard?"

"And I have no plans to join those countrymen of mine who are impoverished to show how much I care about their plight. But I can, we all can, play a part in paving a better road for our people, so that they may share the bounty more fairly."

Maynard walks away from the desk, gesturing his intention to visit the cloakrooms as the three men stay locked in conversation.

"Sounds like Bolshevism to me," says Holmes, with a mischievous grin.

"It's the very opposite," replies Maynard. "My plan promises freedom, not ideological slavery, and fits the capitalist model perfectly – it is based entirely on self-interest!"

They enter the cloakroom, nod to the attendant and as they stand at sparkling porcelain urinals, Maynard sets out his thesis. His rapid-fire words echo off the white tiled walls like a call to arms.

"The present world is no friend to the poor and nor are its laws. Likely as not, they will break them, and if you stand in their way, your skull too. With better distribution of wealth comes less crime, disease and resentment – a more equitable England will be a safer one for us, our friends, children and servants. It is therefore in *our* best interests to invest in the disadvantaged."

As they wash and dry their hands, the one-sided debate continues uninterrupted.

"Oppressive poverty and the riches of Croesus are extremes to be feared – acquisitiveness and greed are base instincts to be risen above. Diogenes tells us to pursue modest pleasure in a state of *ataraxia* – tranquillity and freedom from fear, gained through knowledge of the workings of the world. Aristotle says that personal happiness is more often found in those who have only a moderate share of external goods and Shakespeare agrees…" he says as they swish open the cloakroom door and walk back into the foyer.

"If thou art rich, thou'rt poor;
For, like an ass whose back with ingots bows,
Thou bear's thy heavy riches but a journey,
And only death unloads thee."

Neither man can find flaw in Maynard's logic nor are willing to cross swords further with him for mere sport. Chamberlain brings the conversation to a close with a mumbling dissent about the recent Himalayan rise in income tax and interference of the state. But Maynard's last word is that taxes will deliver a New Jerusalem and that 'free market' politics cannot be trusted with long-term good governance as it will only ever be driven by short-term gain for the few. He pauses before delivering a few quickly concocted faux lines of verse as an encore...

"Of tomorrow, and tomorrow, and tomorrow
They care not, their petty concerns being only for daily profit,
Neither what they bequeath to future times nor
The lessons learnt from our yesterdays enlighten these fools,
They strut their hour upon the stage
And then are heard no more..."

Holmes and Chamberlain look on, wide smiles on their faces as they await the closing of this impromptu soliloquy.

"...The free market is an idiot, full of fury and chaos,
Signifying nothing but dividends at tax-year's end."

They all laugh but by the time they once again stand by the front desk, the conversation has moved back to the Degas auction.

"So now we must now hasten to our briefing at Knoedlers then on to Petit's auction rooms for three o'clock?" says Holmes.

"Before we set off, might I recommend that this would be a good time to don a disguise?" suggests Maynard.

To be certain that Chamberlain is cognizant, Maynard reminds him of the rationale.

"There will be other buyers and the press conducting similar reconnaissance and none should know of the National Gallery's interest — it would attract others to the watering hole, inflate prices and questions would be asked back in England as to the prudence of buying art with Exchequer money."

Chamberlain nods his remembrance of the plan.

"I've brought this rather unflattering deer stalker with me," Maynard then says, taking a hat from his briefcase, unfurling it and handing it to the reluctant Holmes. "And as you rarely wear your spectacles, today you should sport them."

"Do you really think such pantomime necessary?"

Maynard and Chamberlain both nod.

"And tomorrow, for the auction itself, perhaps remove your moustache?" says Maynard.

"I rather hoped we'd forgotten about that."

"It's for the best. England will be grateful for your sacrifice," says Chamberlain, stifling a smile.

It is 1.30 when the three men make their way on foot to the Knoedler art dealership, just a half-mile to the north on rue du Faubourg Saint-Honoré. Outside the streets are still deserted and just a mile to the east, a plume of black smoke can be seen rising up.

Back in London, at Maynard's urging, Holmes had sought instruction on the workings of French auctioneers from Gustavus Mayer at Colnagni in New Bond Street. Then, through his friend Charles Carstairs at the London branch of Knoedler's, Holmes had arranged to receive further guidance from Monsieurs Hamann and Davey, here in Paris. It would be they who would accompany the English raiding party to the Degas sale.

Maynard had initially been wary of Carstairs. Even though his involvement in the project would be at arm's length, the man was an American who had been using European social upheaval and the chaos of war as an opportunity to buy great art works at low prices and spirit them back to the United States. He had bagged one of the great Rembrandt self-portraits for the American industrialist Henry Frick and was on record as saying that "England acquired her great Masterpieces during the French Revolution and Napoleonic Wars and now America's chance had come." Such opportunism was, of course, exactly what Maynard and Holmes were themselves perpetrating.

The Knoedler dealership is housed in a beaux arts building in the heart of the gallery district and its quiet interior and polite, smiling staff are most agreeable. The introductions are completed and pleasantries concluded and both Hamann and George Davey, the man who runs this Paris branch, appear to Maynard like straightforward, trustworthy fellows. Their mission seems to be to assist in whatever way they can. This service will of course be in return for a handsome fee, courtesy of the British Treasury.

12

Galerie George Petit

The Petit Gallery is a further ten minutes' walk away, on the border of the districts of Place Vendome and Concorde. Maynard and Holmes know that although he had inherited the business from his art dealer father Francois, George Petit has established a reputation all his own as a knowledgeable promoter of French Impressionism, a hard-nosed businessman and the possessor of opulent tastes including keeping a string of mistresses and hosting frequent extravagant shooting parties. Maynard has also heard that Petit is ambitious to the point of wanting to ruin his rivals, to drive them out of business, and that his greatest delight is selling art to visiting Americans at four times what it is actually worth. The Petit auction rooms will be a jungle.

After the quintet have walked along the Boulevard de Madeleine and turned the corner of the south-east end of the narrow Rue de Seze, the Galerie Petit comes into view. The five-storey townhouse was built by Petit himself at the beginning of the *Belle Époque* and functions as gallery, sales room and business office. Like many grand Parisian buildings of the 1870s, its façade is of white, travertine limestone in the French Classical style, punctuated with wrought iron ornamental balconies. It is delightful. But in the street outside, things are not as expected. The three Englishmen stop in their tracks, their French assistants too, shocked by what they see.

Whilst the surrounding avenues and streets were deserted, here there are carriages, cars, taxis and a noisy throng around the gallery's entrance. At least two hundred people mill about, either having just left Petit's or are recently arrived. All seem bizarrely oblivious to the threat of the German canon – the atmosphere is more like a garden party than a city under siege. Although the crowd is for the most part elegantly suited gentlemen, there are also ladies in wide-brimmed hats and the latest narrow-bottomed hobble skirts. Others wear head wraps and silk tunics inspired by Bakst's designs for the Ballets Russes, for *The Firebird* and *Petrushka*, which Maynard knows premiered here before the war. One exotic creature has donned a pair of seafoam-green harem trousers and, just as she must have hoped, is turning heads. Even with grave peril in the air, the auction has become a social event and greed has overcome fear as the hordes gather in the hope of acquiring a masterpiece at a bargain price from a once in a lifetime sale.

Holmes, Chamberlain and Maynard exchange demoralised frowns. So much for Maynard's supposition that the chaos of war would mean small attendance and therefore low demand. Inside the stuffy, packed auction rooms, it is difficult to even get close to the pictures. After Hamman and

Davey scuttle off to secure more tickets for the sale tomorrow, Holmes spots other buyers known to him and mutters their names under his breath.

"That's Durand-Ruell acting for the Met' in New York. He's also one of Petit's retained advisers," says Holmes, surreptitiously pointing at a man in his mid-thirties with narrow shoulders and small moustache. "There's Trotti, Hansen of Copenhagen's representative, and that is Paul Leprieur from the Louvre. We're done for. We can forget the feast, we'll be lucky to get crumbs."

Chamberlain removes his monocle, breathes on it and polishes the lens as he throws Maynard a quizzical look. 'And just what do you suggest we do now?' asks his raised eyebrow.

"Let's look at the art," says Maynard, quickly "…in case this is the closest we ever to get to it."

Holmes puts on a brave face and seeks out the first of what would have been his intended purchases. "At least the other collectors haven't recognised me," he whispers under his disguise.

"It's probably worth keeping it that way," says Maynard, behind a fixed smile. "We shall I am sure, be able to afford a few treasures. Not perhaps those that we planned for…"

As his two friends look sceptically at each other, Maynard walks ahead. Before he'd left London, he'd given Meiklejohn, his assistant at the Treasury, a few hundred pounds to set up a bank account in Paris under his own name for personal use. He would collect the cheque book from the

British Embassy tomorrow. It was a perk of privilege of course but he intended to put it to good purpose by rescuing as much great art as possible. At least that's what he tells himself. It won't do his portfolio of investments any harm either.

He pushes gently but determinedly past the other previewers towards a small Still Life oil painting portraying seven green and red apples on a plain background. Yes, this is it. The hand-written descriptor card on the table-top easel confirms it is indeed the Cezanne that Duncan and Nessa had told him to look out for. It is very small, seven inches by five, painted between 1877 and 1878 just before the artist returned to Provence. Maynard remembers that Cezanne had told his Impressionist chums that he'd planned to 'conquer Paris with an apple' and had produced a series of gorgeous studies of this single fruit. Still relatively unknown back in England, perhaps he would now also conquer London. Maynard puts a cross next to *Pomme*, Number 10 in his catalogue, and moves on.

He then identifies two pieces by Delacroix, a dream-like oil called "*Horse Standing in a Meadow*" and a study of the Frieze in the Palais-Bourbon showing the arched tops of classical columns decorated with figures from Greek mythology in graphite and pale watercolour. Both works are wonderful and he determines to make them his if he can.

Maynard catches up with Holmes and Chamberlain as they stand beside an El Greco, a small version of his *San Ildefonso at Illescas* painted around 1600. There's a difference of opinion between the two men and Chamberlain is being uncharacteristically sour.

"You can buy it if you must but I may not sign the cheque," he says with a dismissive wave of his hand as he turns and walks away.

Maynard studies the lurid oil painting of the one-time archbishop, now made a Saint, with its heavy, religious themes and iconography and decides that the subject matter and the opulent excess of its treatment must have gone against the grain of Chamberlain's Liberal politics. There could be no other reason for such a pronounced aversion. Old Masters such as this hadn't been popular for years but Maynard assumes that Holmes wants it because of the lack of El Grecos in the current Trafalgar Square collection.

Maynard reminds himself that Holmes' main purpose here is to help the National Gallery fulfil one of its primary functions – to tell the Story of Art. Holmes' acquisitions will show the viewing public back home how specific techniques evolved, why a particular style developed and how one artist influenced another or sometimes founded an entire artistic movement. As they walk amongst the collection, Holmes explains the importance of the works – why he would have wanted to buy two portraits and a couple of classical fantasies by Ingres because of his influence on the Impressionists. Matisse had described him as the first painter "to use *pure* colours, without distortion." Similarly, Delacroix's expressive brushstrokes informed later styles and so they would have gone after his dining table-sized *Baron Schwiter* made in 1830. They'd have hunted down a four-set of Corot landscapes because he anticipated the *plein-air* innovations of Monet and his Impressionist friends. Holmes also wanted Manet's luminous study of his own wife with a cat on her lap and his six feet by nine *Execution of Maximillian* because the National had so little French art from that period.

And then they come across the Gauguin, ah yes, the Gauguin. The two by two-and-a-half feet sized *Vase of Flowers* from 1896. Red bougainvillea, exotic hibiscus and playful frangipani explode from a black clay pot. Having the same soft edges and textures as much of his other work from Tahiti, it is as if the subject is seen unfocused with eyes half-shut, or as in a dream, the interweaving shapes and patterns casting a spell on the viewer.

"He had little interest in botanical detail – he did not copy nature; that was only his starting point," Holmes explains. "With him, everything important happened in the imagination."

"Whatever else we may miss tomorrow, we must make this ours," says Maynard in pleading tones, looking adoringly at the extravagant bouquet.

"You know that Curzon and other Trustees are not supporters of the Impressionist cause – of Cezanne, Gauguin or even Degas himself? Many of them believe the case for them to be called 'great' is not yet made. But I shall try my best..." replies Holmes, "...as a reward to you for having got me the money."

13

An Evening Stroll

It is just before five-thirty when the demoralised Englishmen leave the gallery, walk south-west across the Place de Madeleine and onto the wide boulevard of the Rue Royal. When they come to Faubourg Saint-Honoré, they thank Messrs Hamman and Davey for their help and bid them *au revoir*. They will meet again tomorrow.

As they set-off for the Crillon, Holmes takes the opportunity to press Chamberlain on conducting further expeditions of this sort in the future, saying that whatever their fortunes may be tomorrow, the National Gallery needs to increase its stock of French art. Chamberlain listens politely but neither agrees or dissents. Maynard walks behind them, only half-listening, but knows that if Chamberlain was unconvinced of the merits of such enterprises, he is even less persuaded now. Holmes is an intelligent, thoughtful sort but has little or no guile.

The politicians have backed this Degas venture because it will secure for the nation, high-value goods at low prices and strike a humiliating blow against the tricksy French and the dastardly Hun. This will play well with the electorate. But now it looks as if they will deliver none of the promised dividends and yet Holmes still requests a repeat performance. What advantage would there be for Chamberlain in supporting the buying of more French art? What measurable benefit would be derived which he could be used to persuade others? If the auction goes against them, as it surely must, Holmes will need new arguments with which to lobby the Machiavellian politicians. They will not be so gung-ho again. Maynard's own stock too will fall and its recovery may be hard and long. His mind now starts to drift. He stops listening to his two friends, lost in other thoughts. When they arrive at the hotel, he announces that he will remain outside for a while, to take a walk.

Maynard catches Holmes's sidelong glance and guesses his concerns.

"Take a care in this troubled place," says Holmes.

"I know well both its charms and its traps," replies Maynard, with a wink. "And I have a pre-conference Council meeting at six-thirty a.m. and need to be early to bed. I shall see you both at dinner."

As Holmes and Chamberlain say their goodbyes and go inside the Crillon, Maynard turns and looks out across the Place de la Concorde. He tidies his hair and straightens his tie. The moon has appeared from behind its concealing clouds and in the soft evening light he strides towards the centre of the park-sized square to view again the Luxor Obelisk at close quarters. As he stares up at the 75 feet high, 3000 year-old yellow granite symbol of fertility, he amuses himself by noting the significance of the pair of circular fountain ponds placed either side of the monument by King Louis-Philippe's engineers at the time of the obelisk's arrival from Egypt and erection in 1833. How beautifully now plays the moon's reflection on the water.

At the Luxor Temple, the original pedestal base had been decorated with four man-sized baboons carved from a single piece of granite. Because they were shown explicitly, grandly sexed and would have offended public decency, the animals, portrayed dancing to welcome the rising of the Sun-God Re, were hidden away in the Louvre. But whether knowingly or not, by including two spherical well-springs of life-giving water next to the monument the project's planners had underscored its phallic nature with something of their own. Maynard is still smiling at the thought of it all when in his peripheral vision, he catches sight of a man, a boy really, about twenty years old, dressed in the horizon-blue uniform of a private in the French army. As Maynard turns to steal a longer look, he can see that whilst the lad is feigning study of the monument, his real interest is, surely, Maynard himself. His many previous joyous Parisian sojourns have taught him it is not only acceptable to flirt with strangers in the street, it is *de rigueur.*

As he becomes more emboldened, Maynard takes time to study the lad's face, his soft-toned skin and *beaux yeux*. He's a stunner and no mistake. And those gorgeous eyes belong to both their mission's mysterious Nurse and to his friend Rachel 'Ray' Costelloe. Maynard believed he had loved her but like young men everywhere when first smitten, hadn't known what to do. It had been exciting and cruel and broken his heart. He'd spent his life almost entirely in the company of other men – at school and then at University, and had no knowledge of the romantic expectations or conventions between the genders. Because Ray wasn't male, he hadn't been able to think of any suitable steps to take. And sex with a woman carried the risk of pregnancy. Outside of honourable betrothal, many of his female social and intellectual equals would have declined on those grounds alone. Then there was that peculiarly English religious and moral guilt to contend with, the decree to remain chaste and free of sin. Shame must be avoided at all costs. What if he would not marry you and word of your congress spread? No decent man would wish to buy a second-hand suit. And so with most acceptable females off-limits, what then are red-blooded boys to do?! It was one of the great ironies of tyrannical Polite Society.

A fellow mathematician and a suffragette, in the end Ray had married Oliver Strachey, Lytton's older brother, in 1911. If she hadn't had children, she'd planned to be an engineer. She was one of the best, most able people he'd ever known and part of him loved her still.

Maynard is still smiling at the memory of her when a strange panic starts to grip him. Did he just glimpse cold menace in the boy-charmer's eyes? He wonders if his proximity to death on the Paris-bound train has caused a partial loss of nerve, but no, he is sure of it. It was the look of a schemer, an agent of harm. Without thinking more, he turns and hurries back towards the Crillon. The building is now in virtual darkness – in blacked-out Paris, light will draw the air-borne dangers of enemy planes and Zeppelins like a moths to a flame.

The boy follows and despite Maynard's quickening stride, stays but five paces behind him. Just yards away from the safety of the foyer and the vigilant hotel doormen, the lad speaks out.

"Attendez monsieur, je ne peux pas vous montrer d'autres curiosités? I know well the *demi-monde. C'est ma ville et je connais bien ses secrets..."*

Maynard doesn't turn around until he is inside. He dabs his moist forehead with his handkerchief and loosens his collar. Looking out into the *Place*, he sees the young soldier wait a few seconds before hurrying away. Then, as if he'd been watching from the shadows of the hotel's colonnade, the male nurse who had accompanied them from Folkestone, appears and follows the boy away in the direction of the Champs-Elysées. The two men disappear into the night.

14

At the Hotel Crillon

Maynard and Chamberlain arrive late for dinner, the Inter-Allied Council meeting having overrun. Apart from half-heartedly joining in a conversation about Seneca's philosophy of food – that the dining table's true function is social, fraternal, rather than culinary, Maynard says little during the meal. Holmes is sure that just as his friend predicted, the Council's deliberations had failed to resolve any of the interest rate disputes with the United States.

After coffee, Holmes, Maynard, Lord Buckmaster, Alfred Booth and Fry are invited to Chamberlain's rooms for a smoke where three French liaison officers and a British General join them. Frederick Sykes is a balding man in his early forties and after Maynard introduces him to Holmes, Sykes explains that although he is presently attached to the Supreme War Council based in Versailles, he is soon to be made Chief of the newly formed British Air Force. Sitting in a blacked-out bay window, the three men exchange pleasantries, pass around cigars and drink more Cognac. The conversation soon moves on to Sykes' impending promotion which although starting cheerily enough quickly brings a look of concern to the military man's face as he speaks of widespread resistance to the formation of a new centralised airborne fighting force, independent of both the army and the navy.

"Projects of great newness are always greeted with suspicion by the unimaginative and with resentment from the lazy on whom the changes are to fall," says Maynard. "All the rest will eye a new plan with scepticism until it is proven to be successful at which point they will claim to have thought it a good idea from the beginning!"

All three chuckle but then Sykes returns to his subject with great seriousness.

"My idea is for a much enlarged, autonomous Flying Corps and in this many see a threat to their own fiefdoms. But air power is the future of armed conflict – he who controls the air will also control the ground and sea beneath."

"You have a vision then," says Maynard, "and that is the difficult part. All you have to do now is implement it."

"Here's to your success, "says Holmes raising a glass, "a forgone conclusion!"

Maynard and Holmes smile but Sykes remains wrapped up in his preoccupations.

"There have been times in this war when we have been losing 10,000 men a day. By the end of the year, there will have been 750,000 British deaths," he goes on. "The wastage, human and economic, of such a stalemate cannot be borne with the fatalistic stoicism which many a callous commander has shown. In future, we must reduce the soldiers in the field who are in the way of harm. Men must be replaced by machines. Fast-moving strikes at selected targets using modern technology – tanks, armoured cars, advanced projectiles like the German super-gun. Aircraft. Stalemates will be broken by the best equipped, the most nimble."

Sykes is about to say more when he suddenly breaks off, catching the eye of Chamberlain as he emerges from his dressing room. It is as if his own words have reminded him of an urgent matter to which he must now attend. He gives Maynard and Holmes his apologies, stands up and bids them goodnight.

"I wonder what that's about?" says Holmes, as they watch Sykes and Chamberlain move out of earshot. "But whatever it is, the time is now ten-thirty and I must adjourn for the night. We both of us have day of some importance tomorrow."

"And I too shall depart," says Maynard, seeing the good sense in Holmes' decision.

134

The two men say their farewells to the group and make to leave but in the doorway of the suite, Chamberlain appears, takes Maynard's arm and holds him gently back.

"If I could have a last word. Sorry," he says, looking at the departing Holmes. "Government stuff I'm afraid. It won't take long."

"Not at all," says Holmes. "I shall see you both at the auction rooms tomorrow afternoon."

Chamberlain ushers Maynard into an adjacent bedroom where to his surprise General Sykes is waiting. Both men look glum.

"The news from the War Council is not good," says Chamberlain, gesturing to Sykes to explain further as he closes the door behind them.

"The Germans are closing in around Amiens, this is on your route home. The town may fall within the next twenty-four hours and they will block the rail track to Boulogne."

Maynard already knows what Sykes is thinking – that the Inter-Ally Council and Holmes should leave now, whilst they still can.

"Our Fifth Army is shattered. We're holding the last of the line of the Somme but don't know for how long," continues Sykes. "It looks as if Foch will be confirmed as Generalissimo so at least there'll now be a single hand on the tiller. But Mr Keynes, your peril is most great."

"General Sykes thinks we should leave Paris immediately and forego both the Finance Mission and the auction," interjects Chamberlain. "I have told him that is impossible. He is doing his duty and we must do ours."

"Quite right," says Maynard. "But thank you for your concern, General."

"Gentlemen, if you remain into tomorrow, the army will no longer be able to protect you. I am sorry, but every officer and man is now needed elsewhere. Your troop escort will be withdrawn."

"So be it and may God be with them," says Chamberlain. "We will have to trust to our own judgement and fortune."

"Then I must say goodnight and good luck," says Sykes, standing up and shaking both their hands. "Let us hope we meet again, in safety, back in London."

After leaving Chamberlain's suite, Maynard doesn't return to his room, instead going downstairs. He first sits in the empty lobby, skimming his way through a half-dozen French magazines before going outside for a smoke. He is tired of course, but restless. He knows he would not be able to sleep yet. Not just yet. He scans what he can see of the Place de la Concorde then stares out beyond, across the Seine, into the dark city, and wonders what passions, jealousies and tenderness might be being shared in its private rooms. But he will not venture out alone again. He has learnt his lesson. In the nearby *Le Jardin de Tuileries*, a dog's bark is quickly silenced.

"I hope you're not considering a late night escapade Mr Keynes," says a voice from the shadows behind him, "to have adventures of a private nature."

Those had been the very words of warning used by Bonar Law back in London. He turns around to see the nurse, her slim body now dressed in plain civilian clothes, a dark raincoat and small, neat Cloche hat, only part of her pretty face visible in the light from the windows behind her. He moves to stand closer to her, intrigued by her presence there at this hour.

"You're out late, Miss…?"

"You may call me Alice."

Maynard nods, her coded message understood.

"I'm sure you're only here for a breath of fresh air, part of your preparation for tomorrow's Council meeting? No-one would wander off into Paris in the middle of the night with such reckless disregard for their own safety," she says with a smile.

"How very perceptive of you," he says with a boyish grin.

"And just what do you talk about at those things? The workings of an International Finance Mission are a mystery to me as is the whole of economics."

"Economics is a mystery to many people, including most economists," he says with a chuckle. "Some see it as a Dark Art, others as philosophy. My friends say I'm just an accountant 'calculating the cheapest way to kill Germans'. They think I'm engineering maximum slaughter at minimum expense.

"And how do you see it?"

"As a science," he answers. "I'm a mathematician by trade – I analyse fiscal metrics which then informs economic policy. One day the science of economics will be as reliable as the science of electricity."

Alice looks sceptical. She is in need of evidence which Maynard, of course, is happy to provide.

"For example, I have observed that consumer expenditure is stable, predictable, somewhere between three-quarters and four-fifths of national disposable income."

"And people save the rest?"

"Yes. Savings which are then used by banks to fund investment to make more goods and services for consumers to buy"

"A circular process, with all the parts in equilibrium..."

Maynard sees he now has her interest. "Ideally," he says.

"Like a healthy body."

"Quite so," he replies, much amused, gently touching her arm.

He is about to continue when the sound of fast-moving footsteps causes them both to look at the hotel entrance where they see two gendarmes stride purposefully up to the doormen and begin to remonstrate.

"Les lumières, putains d'idiots ! Tu sais très bien tirer les stores des fenêtres. Le Kaiser peut voir ces lampes de Berlin et naviguera ici et nous bombardera tous jusqu'à la merde"

The doormen and a foyer porter jump to their black-out duties, begging forgiveness from the fearsome police.

"Pardon monsieur, mademoiselle – mais ces hommes devraient mieux savoir. Le black-out est pour votre protection ainsi que pour les citoyens de Paris," says one of the gendarmes, suddenly noticing Maynard and Alice.

"C'est très bien, vraiment. Merci officier," says Alice, in perfect, accent-free French.

The policemen give short salutes of apology and go on their way, mission complete. The hotel's blinds and curtains are closed now and Maynard and the nurse stand close-by each other under a pale moon, their faces momentarily illuminated as he lights another cigar.

"...and this calculation enables me to model the effects of additional investment, private or public. It is most fascinating," continues Maynard in hushed tones. In the dim light, he can just make out the amusement now playing on her lips at his schoolboy enthusiasm. "I believe it may create a multiplier effect," he says, undeterred, "for every extra pound invested, between three and five additional pounds could be added to the national income - consumers spend more, retailers buy extra for themselves and increase their orders from their wholesalers, who then also spend and invest more."

Behind his words, the underlying math is spiralling through his mind...

dC_w/dY_w is the marginal propensity to consume...$\Delta Y_w = \Delta C_w + \Delta I_w$, where C_w and I_w are the increments of consumption and investment; therefore $\Delta Y_w = k\Delta I_w$, where $1 - 1/k$ is equal to the marginal propensity to consume...call k the investment multiplier...when there is an increment of aggregate investment, income will increase by k times...

"Such growth would instil confidence," he goes on. "Investment by governments in times of unemployment or recession would rebalance a nation's finances and bring prosperity."

She looks at him like a star-struck student who has suddenly understood a new theorem and is dazzled by simple genius of it.

"This will be but a small part of my *Theory of Money*. I shall publish the findings one day and call on Governments to act on them."

"Then you would no longer be a theoretician but an advocate of intervention. You would treat the ailing patient, move from the observations of the scientist to the practical intervention of a clinician – that would be 'politics' would it not?" she says, precociously challenging her tutor.

"If not to improve the condition of the world, then what is the purpose of any science?" he says, drawing in a lungful of cigar smoke. "If something is predictable, it is then controllable. We can moderate its worst excesses and serve our own ethical and political objectives – the good husbandry of a nation's finances to achieve incremental improvement, for the greater good. Economics is a toolkit. The math is merely a means to an end."

"And will it be science or politics which will triumph tomorrow?"

"It is always about the politics," he says with a fatalistic sigh. "Banks in the United States have been lending Britain millions so that we can fight the war. They don't trust our allies, France, Italy, Russia, Belgium and Serbia to repay the loans they need and so we must be their lender. We have put up many assets, British-owned but American-based Securities as collateral."

Maynard pauses to see how all this macroeconomic mumbo-jumbo is going down. He can just make out her cool look as if she is saying "go on, I'm still with you."

"We need more money from the US Government to help us pay back these loans and their Federal Reserve wants the right to cash in our assets should we fail to make the repayments. It's called *subrogation* and we're against it."

"But they would need such security surely?"

"It would give them a stake in our sovereignty – economic pressure to make us dance to their future political tune. But they have to reassure their population that support for us, and them now joining the war, has been a good thing. Receiving a financial windfall like this one will help them to do this. They have their pressures too."

She nods, acknowledging the conundrum.

"It is part of the Gordian knot we shall try to untie tomorrow. You see, economics is always politics."

"And I'm just a humble nurse, thank God."

Maynard gives her an amused, knowing look then flicks the ash from his cigar.

"Who also knows all about our little art raid I'll wager?"

She replies with a smile which says, 'of course'.

"Bonar Law sent you," he whispers to her. "You're one of Cummings' lot? The Secret Intelligence Service, Section 1C..."

She turns away and lights a cigarette.

"So tomorrow you'll buy art at bargain prices and spirit it back to England where it'll sit in a vault somewhere," she says.

"Only until the war is over. Then the National Gallery will put it on display for the whole country to see. Those pictures are my real mission here. When peace returns, our nations' cultural vault will be most needed and art is food for the public soul. Its contemplation gives rise to states of mind which are good – art is inspiration, redemption, transfiguration. It will help keep people from war. I have told you about my *Theory of Money*, well this is my *Theory of Beauty*."

"I don't believe a Still Life by Cezanne can save us from the devil."

"But you must! Great art is the Holy Water of healing. I'm agnostic, but it is God's gift to us."

She says nothing for few moments, drawing thoughtfully on her cigarette.

"And I will try to help your quest my brave, foolish Don Quixote," she says finally, resting her hand gently on his arm.

"Thus far you have succeeded very well," he says, taking her hand, but made suddenly awkward by her caring smile. "We're safely here in Paris and you've managed to keep me talking long enough so that all thoughts of adventure are dispelled. Now it's time for bed."

"It's all part of the service, Mr Keynes. You may be here to change lives but I am here to save them, yours included."

They look at each other for a few seconds longer than they intended and just as he is about to say goodnight, perhaps even steal a kiss, she returns to business.

"Did you see Nurse Taylor earlier this evening? He was with us on the journey down from Folkestone."

"Yes, at around six. He was here at the front of the hotel then set off in the direction of the Champs-Élysées, why?"

"We haven't seen or heard from him."

"Perhaps he's lucky enough to be out enjoying the fleshpots of Paris?"

"That's not his style. He can look after himself but we're worried. The city is full of danger – spies, agents, assassins, preparing the ground for the invasion…" she says, biting her lip as she stares out into the gloom "…the Germans will overrun us I fear. The city will fall."

She treads out her cigarette, smooths down the sides of her skirt then as she walks away, bids him goodnight.

Maynard is about to re-enter the hotel when he stops in his tracks. He really should explain everything to her, how young Taylor was following someone suspicious and may now be in peril. He turns to speak to her but she has gone.

15

The Auction

For the now clean-shaven Charles Holmes, the morning of Tuesday the 26th March will pass slowly. After breakfast, Maynard leaves him alone, rushing off to his Council meeting in a mood of irritability, anticipating the negotiations will be yet another unseemly display of self-serving brinkmanship. But Holmes has his own ordeal to endure.

The Degas sale will not begin until two o'clock and so he will spend the intervening time at Knoedlers going over etiquettes and techniques, the do's and don'ts of Fine Art auctioneering; all courtesy of MM. Hamann and Davey. Holmes has attended only a few auctions before and they were modest London affairs where he knew most of the other bidders. This would be very different. The sums involved here are great and he will lead a team, the National team, and be part of a grand subterfuge. The nerves in his face and hands already tingle when he thinks of what is to come.

It is nine-thirty a.m. when he sits down in Monsieur Davey's office at Rue du Faubourg Saint-Honoré and reminds himself that when being tutored in a subject about which one already knows quite a lot, maintaining concentration can be difficult. The mind of the listener tends to wander off into distraction and therefore miss important new information. It can also be hard filleting out the known from the unknown as both can be within the same sentence. He resolves to do his best to remain alert and show polite gratitude at all times. So his tutorial begins. Mercifully, it is conducted in English:

Firstly, Davey says, they must watch out for collusion: two or more other parties may have agreed not to bid against each other so as to keep prices artificially low. This can indicate that the Lot is much sought-after and therefore Holmes should be ready to bid high.

He should note the increments by which the bids are increasing. That can tell him what the opinion of both the crowd and the auctioneer is as to the merit of the piece.

Always wait for the opening bids to come from the floor in order to gauge interest. If no offers come, particularly if previous lots were generating much excitement, it could be that there's a problem with the piece which you don't know about.

If Holmes wants to frighten off random bidders and show that he's determined to get the piece, he should be pushy. Make his next bid immediately after his opponent.

But if he wants to stalk his prey, he should behave hesitantly – leave it until the last second before bidding. This can suggest that you either don't care or that have strong doubts about the piece. It can be a useful ploy if you're prepared to get the picture at any price.

If there are two active bidders, stay out of it until one drops out then make your move. The remaining opponent may well be surprised by your late intervention when they thought they'd won. This can wrong-foot and demoralise your adversary which will undermine their confidence and judgement.

Do not show weakness by extending your pause time between bids as the sums increase. This shows your opponent that you are nearing your ceiling and that it should therefore be easy to squeeze you out by making just one or two more bids.

Don't be surprised if the auctioneer moves at random through the catalogue. He may wish to show-off the minor lots in case some people having got the big fish they'd come for are thinking of leaving. It also keeps the attention of all the buyers in the room.

Holmes is with them so far and is confident he has retained their advice for use this afternoon. Davey and Hamann then invent imagined auction scenarios which are played out to test their student's understanding. Lastly, they quiz Holmes about the contents and order of pieces in the Degas catalogue. Questions on the likely values of various pieces, taken out of catalogue-order, are fired off at random intervals and designed to unnerve him. They want to see if he will keep his good judgement under pressure. He passes the examination.

Then they go back to the beginning of the lesson and start all over again. And so it goes on. For three hours. Even luncheon is seen by the Hamann and Davey double-act as an opportunity to test their student's memory. The whole business results in an uncomfortable episode of indigestion for the Director of the National Gallery and by the time they arrive at the Galerie George Petit at one-thirty, he is exhausted and nauseous. When the stakes are this high, auction craft is a mixture of Poker, Bridge and Chess – bluff, disguise, playacting, street-market haggling and horse-trading. Holmes has little aptitude for any of these things and as they sit in an unoccupied corner of the sale-room his already anxious heart sinks still further. He feels the rival bidders are eyeing him with a mixture of suspicion and contempt. He has the words 'OUT OF MY DEPTH' written in bold capitals across his reddening, taut face. He starts to panic, fearing he will make a hash of it, be publicly sliced and diced and the baying crowd will delight in the cruel spectacle. He knows too that the foreign correspondents of the *American Art News*, the *New York Herald*, *Le Figaro* and *The Times,* are there in the crowd and that they will soon recognise him and laugh loudly at his pathetic attempts to disguise himself.

The minutes tick by and he remembers that Maynard is a fine chess player and that his Knoedler tutors are also there to help. He knows they will give good guidance. He prays they will. It is now almost two o'clock and Maynard and Chamberlain are not yet arrived. Wait, yes, there they are. Thank God. They wave at him and push through the throng to the seats he has retained on their behalf. The room is now full to bursting.

Through a doorway at the back of the sale room, Jacques Dubourg, the auctioneer appears and is greeted with applause. He is quickly joined on the podium by the bearded, louche, Monsieur Petit himself and together they smile and bask in the crowd's attention. As Petit sits down, Duborg takes his place at the lectern and an excited, tense murmuring of anticipation fills the room. At two p.m. precisely, proceedings begin in the *middle* of the catalogue. This has Chamberlain and Maynard frantically turning the pages and Davey catches Holmes' eye as if to say, 'I warned you this might happen.' Holmes takes a moment to explain the reasons for these strange manoeuvres but both men stare back at him perplexed. The first three Lots are dealt with rapidly as the auctioneer jumps around taking the works completely out of sequence. Maynard frowns and points at Roger Fry's estimates as first a Gauguin and then a Corot sketch are sold for twice the anticipated price. Maynard is agitated and shifts uncomfortably in his seat.

Things are playing out as he had feared and he leans in towards Holmes to speak quietly into his ear.

"This is my fault. All these people, so many buyers – it was the most horrible miscalculation. But we must try to salvage something from the wreckage and return home with a treasure, however overpriced. Our twenty-thousand might at least buy us respectable failure."

He conveys the same message to Chamberlain who responds with a shrug as if confirming his long-held doubts about the wisdom of the plan. The mood of the three men is further depressed when over the next forty minutes, they are presented with an interminable line of minor works in which they are not the slightest bit interested. But then Holmes relaxes, accepting of the fate of their mission. With the burden of expectation lifted from his shoulders, he uses the bidding to get accustomed to the ways and voice of the auctioneer and to speed up his currency conversion skills – Francs to Sterling at twenty-seven to the Pound. He even tries his hand at going for things he does not really want and the effort, though mercifully unsuccessful, does at least build his confidence to join in when their targets are finally put on the easel. After nearly an hour though, the paintings they have been waiting for have still not appeared.

"I almost hope they don't materialise," says Maynard. "It'll be like watching one's true love sail away with a rich rival. I don't think I can bear it."

These words have just left his lips when, at exactly three o'clock, a dull 'boom' sounds in a nearby street. A few minutes later, another is heard, this time closer. There had been no warning, no sound of aircraft overhead, no siren nor any sound of gunfire before the explosions.

The room falls silent then the dreaded words begin to circulate, *"C'est le canon."*

The Englishmen know the truth of it too, it is the *Emperor William* gun. Many in the room exchange nervous glances then a quarter of the crowd button their jackets, stand up and leave. Nothing more happens for five minutes and few words are spoken. The auctioneer announces a pause in proceedings and walks out. Then, at three-fifteen, a third 'boom' is heard, louder, closer than before. The building vibrates. Of the room's two hundred original occupants, at least seventy had left after the first explosions and now a hundred more join what quickly becomes a rush for the doors. Maynard and Holmes look at each other, not daring to smile, but only thirty or so bidders now remain. If they keep their nerve, and if the auction continues, prices will fall and the day may yet be theirs.

Maynard's mind is now racing. What is going on behind the scenes? The auctioneers will be in fraught conversation with the bourgeois, acquisitive Degas family and their advisers. The French Government may be involved, concerned about the possible destruction of the art but also worried about the loss of much-needed sales taxes if the event is cancelled. If they abandon the sale and a shell were to hit the building, the art and its profits

152

will be lost and no insurer would provide. If they continue, values will certainly be reduced and the lives of the Petit staff would be risked. But at least if paintings were now sold, at the moment the hammer hits the block, the art would no longer be the family's responsibility and the money would be theirs.

After ten more nerve-jangling minutes, without announcement, the auctioneer reappears and the first of the paintings which Holmes and Maynard have been so impatiently waiting for is manhandled onto the display easel at the front of the room. It is Ingres' portrait of the severe-looking soldier-diplomat and Chief of Police in Rome, *Monsieur de Norvin*. As final adjustments are made to the picture's position and the few prospective bidders left fall silent, the auctioneer reminds the room of the history of the piece – that it dates from 1812 and is a unique innovation. Ingres used oil paint in a pure, flat manner, almost like gauche. The perspective too is flattened, eliminating the depth of traditional early nineteenth-century painting. And there is more to this work than first meets the eye. Norvin was a supporter of Napoleon and this allegiance is conveyed by his left hand being placed inside his jacket. The painting had originally shown a bust of the Emperor's infant son on the shelf behind the sitter but following the fall of Bonaparte in April 1814, Ingres had hastily repainted parts of the canvas to conceal the sculpture. He had also reworked the man's collar to conceal his Napoleonic ribbons and lowered the head to make the subject look less autocratic. As the oil paint had thinned over time, the bust and the other changes were becoming visible as ghostly outlines. Then, with the auctioneer's introduction over, the bids begin.

"Quarante mille."

"Quarante deux mille."

"Quarante-deux mille cinq cents."

"Quarante-sept mille francs…aller une fois…deux fois…vendu!"

The bidding is rapid, brief and in the echoing room, involves little competition. Holmes secures the painting for one third of the price they had expected to pay.

Next, the life-sized portrait of *Baron Schwiter* by Delacroix is brought to the front of the sales room. Showing Louis-Auguste Schwiter, a fellow artist and friend of Delacroix as an elegantly dressed figure in an outdoor parkland setting, the subject's face has the delicate cast of melancholia. The pale-skinned, slim, Byronesque figure posed against a muted evening sky and sombre landscape, conveys poetic isolation and its inherent sadness strikes Maynard with greater poignancy than it had done at the preview. On this acquisition though, Holmes has competition. The Louvre's Paul Leprieur has remained behind in the dwindled crowd and is seated directly in front of the easel. He looks intent on securing his prize.

"Like the National, the Louvre have nothing by Delacroix. They will kill to get it," whispers Holmes.

"And if we don't get it, Duncan and Nessa will kill us!" replies Maynard behind his hand.

Amongst the French mutterings going on around them, Maynard hears that some of the crowd suppose all five of them are working for Knoedlers on behalf of a wealthy American collector or that perhaps Chamberlain, Maynard and Holmes are rich Americans themselves. This is to the Englishmen's advantage. The other bidders will think they cannot compete and so will quickly give up. Maynard is also greatly relieved that Holmes' disguise has worked for if the Louvre suspects for one moment that it is the National Gallery they bid against, they will know that funds are limited and will keep raising the price, confident of winning. French pride would also demand the works be prevented from crossing the Channel at any cost – wherever else the paintings might end up, it must not be England. Should a single painting be lost to Trafalgar Square, their jobs would quickly follow.

After three rounds of bidding against the still anonymous Holmes, Leprieur begins to sweat, at times twisting and straining to see who is daring to battle against the esteemed national gallery of France. But Holmes refuses to be intimidated and presses on. The one-upmanship between them continues, to-and-fro like gladiatorial tennis players exchanging raking ground shots over the net with neither giving ground. A hubbub begins to build and the partisan French amongst the crowd crane to see the face of the disrespectful would-be pillager of their nation's artistic heritage.

With the bidding parked at 70,000 francs in Holmes' favour, Leprieur stands up and livid and red-faced, shouts across the room.

"C'est pour le Louvre, Monsieur."

Others in the crowd join in, decrying and deriding, trying to scare off the poacher.

"Vous luttez contre le Louvre Monsieur, contre le Louvre."

The clamour builds into hisses, boos and shouts of abuse. Holmes is starting to feel clammy, nauseous, he is almost sick – unsure of what to do next. But he knows that if he falters, shows any outward signs of giving-way, the picture will be lost to them. He reasons it is better to face down the hounds now than live with his own regret for funking. He is taken back two nights, to their Paris-bound train and the bombing of Amiens, with adversity surging around him. Now, as then, he steels himself and the fear is kept at bay. After two more rounds of bidding, he secures the prize for 80,000 francs, around £3,200, a most acceptable price.

The painting has an ornate eight-inch wide gilt frame of coiled leaves and flowers and Maynard is already thinking it will be the devil's own job to get it home. Still no one has yet recognised Holmes. They can proceed.

Maynard gives Holmes' a congratulatory pat on the arm and explains to him in hushed whispers that the crowd think the three of them work for Knoedlers or are visiting Americans, there under the protective wing of Hamann and Davey.

"…to them we are brash interlopers with little knowledge of art or sale room etiquette," he says quietly as the other bidders chatter, awaiting the next Lot. "They will neither trust our judgement nor predict our behaviour," he says, gripping Holmes' arm triumphantly. "We've kissed them, let us now take them to bed!" Holmes winces a little as he smiles at Maynard's coarse allusion but then nods his intention to press on with gusto.

The next Delacroix though, *Count Mornay's Apartment*, gets away from them, sold to the Louvre for 22,000 Francs. Holmes says it is pleasant enough but certainly not worth chasing above the upper limit price Hamann and Davey have suggested. The Louvre have overpaid, it is a misjudgement, they are rattled.

Then the big Manet appears, or rather the pieces of it. There are a series of paintings titled *The Execution of Maximillian* and this is the 1867 version, damaged after hanging neglected for months in Manet's studio. His family had cut away the ruined sections leaving it in four pieces and Degas had gone to great pains to track down and reassemble what was left of the picture onto a single six-foot by nine canvas. It depicts the real-life killing of Maximillian I, the French puppet ruler of Mexico, by revolutionary soldiers and it was thought that in painting such a scene, Manet was letting the flag of his Republican sympathies be unfurled. Holmes scoops it for 23,000 francs.

Over the next hour, he gets *Femme avec un chat* – Manet's wife with her cat, dating from 1880, followed by three more paintings by Ingres as well as four of his sketches. He also bags works by Rousseau, Forain, Ricard, ten Delacroix sketches and Corot's gorgeous little landscape showing the *Ruins in the Roman Capagna*. Finally, and to Maynard's great delight, Holmes secures Gauguin's *Vase of Flowers*.

But when Cezanne's *Apples* are placed on the easel, Holmes cannot be persuaded. Perhaps he is sated. But the problem swiftly becomes Maynard's opportunity and he seizes the moment. Over the next ten minutes, he himself becomes an art collector. He not only makes off with the Cezanne at £360 but then, as the final Lots of the day are offered to just a dozen remaining buyers, he also captures a delicious graphite and white chalk nude by Ingres and two Delacroix paintings – the *Horse Standing in a Meadow* and the *Study of the Bourbon Frieze*. As soon as the hammer hits the block and the latter is his, he decides, he knows not why, that he will gift it to Duncan.

As the auction is brought to an end, Maynard idly calculates the value of £360 one hundred years hence. Based on current inflation rates and their likely fluctuations, the national purchasing power index and wage growth, he estimates that its price tag would be an incredible £80,000. But that is mere bagatelle. Before they left London, he examined the growth of Fine Art as an asset class in its own right and if his back-of-envelope assumptions were proved right then by the year 2018, his little bowl of apples would be worth fifteen million pounds! The sober Keynes, the economist and academic, scoffs at the ludicrousness of such a sum. The acquisitive opportunist in him grieves that he won't be there to cash-in his investment. He chuckles away his musings and turns to Holmes and Chamberlain with a broad smile of triumph.

"Well, you pulled it off," says Chamberlain.

"*We* pulled it off," says Maynard insistently, grinning like Lewis Carroll's Cheshire cat.

"When Maynard is involved, positive outcomes are usually assured," Holmes adds. "He's a lucky general."

It is a bitter-sweet remark and the smiles of the five men are rendered less wide by this reminder of their peril. The danger of more shelling is real but it does not cast too dense a pall over their mood as they return to the Crillon. They give their thanks to Davey and Hamann halfway down the Rue Royale and by the time they enter the hotel foyer, they are once again jovial and looking forward to meeting for celebratory pre-dinner drinks. But the place is quiet, deserted actually. Few if any uniformed army officers are in sight and no other guests mill around. At the desk, only one clerk is visible and he is chattering in hushed tones into a telephone. As they walk towards the grand staircase, they see Geoffrey Fry sitting ashen-faced in an armchair reading French newspapers. He stands up quickly as if he has been waiting for them.

"Thank God you're all safe. You heard the explosions I am sure – shells from the monster gun have been landing all over Paris, two of them not a hundred yards from here. One of Sykes' Adjutants told me that the Germans have broken through our lines – the army is overwhelmed and in desperate retreat. The Hun have split the British and French armies in two and are raging through the gap. They say the French are still fighting like tigers at Noyon but Paris is now threatened. The Government is to retire to Bordeaux."

16

Night Moves

Chamberlain and Fry are thinking the same thing. Whilst they must stay until tomorrow night to finish their vital Council business, Holmes should, must, be allowed to flee. Holmes himself prays the others cannot detect his faintheartedness for part of him also wishes to leave. But his resolute self demands once again that he faces his fear and returns to the auction rooms tomorrow. There is great art yet to be captured and he must at least try to win some of it for the nation.

The four men stand in silence for a few seconds. Looking down at the newspaper on the seat where Fry had been sitting, Holmes asks "Does it say if Debussy was killed by the great gun?"

The others frown, they have more pressing concerns than the death of a composer. But Maynard knows that Holmes' posing of such an irrelevance is not dissimilar to his own self-distracting musings during the shelling of their train at Amiens. He affords himself a little smile at the strange irrationality of such displacement behaviours but says nothing about it.

"No, by a cancer..." explains Fry, "...at his home off the Avenue du Bois de Boulogne. He'd been suffering for a number of years apparently. Oh, and another musician, Lilli Boulanger, is dead too."

Holmes is saddened by the news and he knows his wife will be much upset. The world is falling apart around him.

"I think Mr Holmes should return to England," Fry goes on, turning to the other two. "I can get him onto a north-bound train this evening."

"How far away are the Hun?" asks Chamberlain.

"Fifty miles. If they move much further cross-country, they'll cut off our escape route to the Channel. The Adjutant said the German charge is led by Storm Troopers – their most experienced fighters; fast-moving, skilled, merciless."

"Then the Director of the National Gallery must be got home," says Chamberlain.

"And what of the paintings?" asks Maynard.

"What has already been bought can be loaded-up and taken back to London. *You* can go back to the auction room tomorrow to buy whatever's left on the shopping list," says Chamberlain.

Maynard now speaks calmly but forcefully. "If we are to complete our mission then Holmes must remain another day. I know insufficient about the artworks to expend our country's money on them and too little about auction craft to direct Hamann and Davey."

162

"I want to stay," pleads the now resolute Holmes. "You'll all be here until the Council finishes its business and I need to complete my business too. You cannot ask me to run. I would be abandoning both friends and duty."

"How much money remains unspent?" asks Fry.

"Around six thousand pounds – a little more than one quarter of the original Grant," says purse-warden Chamberlain.

The four men look at each other but no one speaks. Then they all nod in agreement. Holmes will stay. Maynard smiles.

They are now running late and Maynard and Holmes wash and dress for dinner hurriedly. By seven-thirty, they are sat in a private, mirrored dining room amongst the Inter Ally Council members and a group of French liaison officers. They both try to forget their imminent peril but when they think of it, are resolute. It will take more than the proximity of an army of Huns to disrupt an Englishman's mealtime.

The euphoria of their day's triumphs quickly returns and both men chink their glasses together and quaff Champagne topped up with Cognac. They will go back to the auction rooms tomorrow, bag yet more booty then return to London in triumph. Bombing raids and shelling had not stopped them nor had long-barrelled guns and neither now will advancing German hoards. They are fated to succeed.

The young Adjutant, a Captain Tyndale-Atkinson, who had been sent by General Sykes from Versailles to alert Fry and the other British guests at the Crillon as to their peril is present and now shares his news with those at his end of the table.

"Clemenceau has made Foch the Generalissimo – he will be our Commander-in-Chief," he announces. "The War Council met at Doullens Town Hall and agreed that he will develop the strategy for all allied troops."

"And suppose he cannot implement it in time – if the Germans move on Paris, will the city's defences hold?" asks Maynard.

"So far, we have been unable to stop their Storm Troopers. I have heard that they move from shell-hole to shell-hole in leaps and bounds, through fire, staying close to the earth like animals, never forfeiting intent, ever self-reliant and resourceful. They answer every blow with a counter blow. They are a new kind of man from a manly caste. A fighter caste..."

The young Adjutant begins to falter before rallying then re-commencing, his words slower and more hesitant.

"...our only hope is that the speed of their advance will outstrip their own supply lines – that the attack will peter out."

None in the group speak. Maynard and Holmes look at each other, reminded that their fate and that of the city hangs in the balance.

"I regret to say that the gap between the French and British armies which the Hun now exploits is a manifestation of the long-standing gulf between the respective sets of politicians and generals," observes Maynard, finally breaking the heavy silence.

"Yes, even within our own High Command, there are divisions on both tactics and Foch's appointment," agrees the Adjutant.

"Mercifully, our forces are now under a single unifying command. Let us hope it is not too late," says Holmes, raising another glass.

"I am pleased you have confidence in our General Foch who will now command your British officers," interjects a young French Officer who has been sitting close to their group. He speaks English in a crisp, precise manner as he moves the conversation on. "And most respected sir, what is your opinion of the man who appointed him, of Clemenceau, our Prime Minister?" he says, focusing on Maynard.

"Well, Monsieur…?"

"Lieutenant Guy Leconte, at your service," says the young man deferentially.

"In my dealings with him, I have found that he has little interest in, or indeed grasp of, close detail but then he doesn't need to have."

"I hope you do not malign him, Monsieur?" says Leconte. The young man is still subservient in his manner but his expression is now laced with defensiveness. "We believe in him the way our ancestors believed in Joan of Arc."

"And rightly so. His job is to inspire, to lead, to take far-reaching decisions, not to busy himself with exactitudes, he has not the time. His duty is to put other people in place to deal with such fine grain." Maynard pauses to take another gulp of wine then leans forward as he warms to this new debate. "He visits the frontline trenches often to speak to his soldiers I hear, to let those brave men know their government is looking after them. He is one of them and they know that if necessary, he will die as one of them."

"Yes, and these are not gestures of empty worth, he fought many duels in his youth," says Leconte. "He has the heart of a lion."

"And his troops know this through the courage of his words. A transcript of a speech he gave was circulated to our Cabinet. He talked of the idea of Total War and the policy of *'la guerre jusqu'au bout'* – 'war until the end.' It left quite an impression on members of our government, on Mr Churchill, our Minister of Munitions in particular."

"Ah, I saw Monsieur Winston on Thursday last, just before the German bombardment began, at Nurlu near Cambrai," says Leconte, quite casually. "He was visiting your General Tudor at the front. The whole area was overrun the next day. I hope he was able to escape in time."

Maynard is greatly taken aback and exchanges looks of concern with Holmes.

"My God, yes, I believe he was in France to discuss the delivery of tanks with Haig and Birch, the chief of Artillery, and to attend a Chemical Warfare Conference at Saint Omer," Maynard says. "Your news is most troubling. Like or loathe his politics, I believe Winston to be a man of profound destiny. If he has been lost, England's future may take on a different shape."

"Do not worry, I am certain he is safe and if so, he will surely come here. The Crillon and the Ritz are his favoured hotels in Paris."

"From what I know of him, he would have wished to stay to fight. Like Clemenceau, he still regards himself as a soldier."

"And thus brave Churchill and Clemenceau will be the Fathers of our Victory," Leconte continues, cheerily raising his glass as he tries to lift their spirits.

"Yes, I believe they will," agrees a once again smiling Maynard, as they toast to the common endeavour. He catches the look in Holmes' eye and realises they have already had too much to drink.

The next hour passes in jovial mood as Holmes and Maynard extract stories from the young soldiers about life at the Front, the entertainments of Paris nightlife and some of the less seemly goings on here at the Hotel Crillon. As the wine flows, Leconte also asks questions – about London, the current Inter-Ally negotiations and their success today at the Galerie George Petit. "I have heard that you emptied Paris of all its great art in a single hour!" he says, smiling. "My congratulations, but I hope you have left a few morsels on which we French may feed. You are not planning to raid also our Louvre I trust?!"

"The scale of our endeavours has been greatly exaggerated," says Holmes. "We have secured only a few carefully chosen pieces – works which will fill the gaps in our own poor National collection. But we hope to get one or two more tomorrow."

Maynard looks askance at this *faux pas* and is suddenly made nervous. If Leconte knows of their mission, then by tomorrow so might many others. Their rivals at the auction will realise who they are.

"Indeed?" says Leconte, becoming more intrigued. "Perhaps then I may be of some assistance prior to your return to the front line of the auction room?"

Maynard lights a cigarette but says nothing.

167

"I know of another fine collection in a private house on the Avenue du Bois de Boulogne, but a few minutes away by taxi from here. Many of the works there are also for sale."

"And could you take us to this Aladdin's cave? We would be in your debt," said Holmes enthusiastically.

Tyndale-Atkinson now wears a look of polite nervousness and Maynard reads the Adjutant's thoughts in an instant. Yes, they would be with a French Liaison Officer whose judgement and character he would have trusted, up to a point, but if a situation of danger arose...

"We would be most interested to see these treasures," says Holmes, his eyes now sparkling with anticipation.

"Then I will use the telephone to book your visit. Shall we say ten at o'clock?"

"Yes, thank you," says Holmes, looking at Maynard for confirmation that it this not too rushed an arrangement. Maynard nods his agreement.

Leconte stands up and hurries away to make his call but as soon as he is out of sight, Tyndale-Atkinson makes his apologies and also rises from his seat. Maynard watches the Adjutant ask a waiter a question then walk off towards the lobby. Is he going to make a phone call himself and if so, to whom?

Leconte returns to confirm that all is now arranged then sits by patiently whilst Maynard and Holmes finish their desserts. Foregoing coffee and brandy, the three make their apologies and go back to their respective rooms before reconvening in the hotel lobby. Five minutes later, in the taxi

which will take them north-west along the Champs Elysees in the direction
of the Bois du Boulogne, Maynard catches sight of their party's doctor
speaking to Tyndale-Atkinson in the foyer. The young Adjutant is drawing
his attention to their departure with a stabbing finger. They are worrying
unnecessarily, Maynard thinks.

As their cab makes its way along the wide avenues, a now somewhat worse-
for-wear Maynard looks out of the window and in his blurred mind,
contents himself with the knowledge that whilst tonight's expedition would
likely be a tame affair without the possibility of any interlude, it will not be
long before he would be back on home turf. In London, the streets, theatre
bars and late night train carriages are his, a world of shadows and sweetness
in the dark. For his part, Holmes believes this is the most tipsy he has been
for many a year but resolves to pull him himself together.

The thoroughfare of the Bois du Boulogne is more than fifty yards wide
and is separated from the parallel access roads which serve its palatial
properties by wide promenades and grassy strips planted thick with trees.
The taxi turns off the main boulevard and drives past the embassies and
grand apartment buildings until the Liaison Officer tells the driver to stop.
Looking out, Holmes and Maynard are reassured their visit will not be in
vain – any art collection housed in such surroundings will be most worthy
of their attention. But after Leconte leads them through a set of ornate
gates, he takes them not to the front door of the main house but along a
side path to a shabby annex at the rear of the grounds, the roof and

stonework of which look in urgent need of attention. The door is opened by an old manservant in an ill-fitting uniform who sullenly ushers them through a hallway and into a dimly-lit, six-sided room with walls covered in paintings. The servant begs them wait before returning with glasses of whisky laced with soda.

The art is most underwhelming and Holmes now eyes Leconte with increasing suspicion. There are one or two pleasant things; an early work by Rousseau, a Huet and a Millet and two framed sketches by Daubigny. All fall into the 'minor works' category and none are a patch on what they have just acquired. Leconte is standing back, observing the Englishmen as they discuss the merits and otherwise of the pictures now before them when silently, through a seamless panel in a wall, a rotund, pale-skinned man in his mid-fifties appears. He has a pencil-line moustache and brilliantined hair and is wearing a bright blue smoking jacket and cream and brown two-tone shoes.

"Good evening, gentlemen. I am sorry that you are kept waiting. I am the owner of this most meritorious collection," he says in perfect English. Holding a suitably large cigar, the man offers a ham-sized hand of greeting first to Holmes and then to Maynard. "I see you have drinks. That is good. And do see a work which particularly delights you?"

"It is hard to choose one over another, they are all very wonderful, Monsieur...," says Holmes. Both Maynard and their spherical host can see that he is lying.

"I am Count Vizsla, but I do not use my name beyond these walls," says the big fellow as he takes Holmes gently by the arm and leads him along the line of paintings. "The authorities are making very much trouble for me – tax collectors, brigands who will take my riches for themselves. Soon they will raise the rate again to steal more money from me than before. Thieves, all thieves…"

"Yes, the art tax in our country can be punitive. Many transactions are carried out abroad in an attempt to circumvent…" begins Holmes, before Vizsla interrupts him.

"What about this small delight, a Corot? It may have escaped your attention," says the Count, pointing at a tiny landscape painting of a hay wagon in a setting of trees and fields.

"We acquired a number of his works just today and so sadly…"

"Then perhaps more modern canvases will please you…" he says, suddenly giving up on Holmes to turn to Maynard. "…some of which may be of great interest."

Maynard nods enthusiastically, but then looking to Holmes for support, realises his friend has long since given up on the prospect of finding anything of merit. Holmes' nerves are now beginning to jangle. Have they been brought here so that harm can be done to them? He is rapidly sobering up even if Maynard is not.

"Please, gentlemen, follow me," says Vizsla as he leads the way back into the hall and along a narrow corridor to an under-stairs door. Down a dozen steps and along a dank, dark passage way, Maynard reasons they must now be under the main house and that this is part of its maze of cellars. Once through another door, the Englishmen find themselves in a great windowless room hung with more art. Holmes recognises some of the pictures – they are by Braque, Dufy and Matisse and much of it is in the style of the *Fauve* group of painters, the so-called *Wild Beasts*. As Maynard gazes around in amazement, the words of one art critic come back to him – "a pot of paint has been flung in the face of the public." Quite so. But there is something else here too.

Some are known as 'Cubists', yes, he thinks that is their name. They portray human figures and still life objects as geometric shapes, shown from different viewpoints but all at the same time. As he looks at one of the paintings – an almost two-foot square oil in browns, greys and whites, of a small stringed instrument, broken into a hundred fragmented pieces, he suddenly understands. It is incredible. No longer tied to one single perspective, the artist can now create three-dimensionality. We are all of us multifaceted and now freed from the absolutism of right and wrong, this art shows how we must see ourselves and others – as complex creatures with many faces who, even within a single lifetime, may lead many different lives.

The rest of the canvases are also most daring – riots of bold, bright colour, where static conventionality has been swept away. These works are dynamic, they move, and many are lit-up by the burning sun of the French south and North Africa. This is a revolution and once again, France is at its epicentre. The overthrow of tyranny and the creation of *La Republique,* the Declaration of the Rights of the Citizen, Impressionism's challenge to the stuffy protocols of the Paris Salon and the *Ecole des Beaux-Arts*, and now it will nurture the burgeoning Modern world. Cubism is a vision of the future and like its protagonists, Maynard determines to be part of the brave new epoch. Modernism will be the birth of Now.

"This is by Signor Picasso, a Spaniard," says the Count, sweeping across to a large abstract – a collision of angular forms of bottles and more musical instruments, painted in silver and muted red-brown.

'Picasso, yes, I may have met him,' thinks Maynard. 'In Ottoline's garden at Garsington.' Damn, if only he'd paid more attention, he could have bagged a bargain.

"But perhaps the most beautiful are these by the young master Matisse," says Vizsla with a flamboyant flourish as he moves swiftly on, waving his hand in front of a line of smaller oils. "One day he will be known to the whole world and his works will bring fortunes to their owners. Only men such as ourselves can see this. You will agree my Lord Maynard, the critics, the fools of the Conservatoires, cannot know this truth of course. But they will regret their prejudice. And so will their bank managers," he adds, tittering.

"I'm no Lord, only a Knight Companion…like a Chevalier of your *Legion of Honour*," says Maynard frowning, alarmed by the knowledge this stranger seems to have of him and, he presumes, of Holmes too. He reasons that Leconte must have marked the man's card.

"It is not *my* Legion of Honour, I am not French," says Vizsla, pursing his lips together. Maynard nods and smiles back politely. "And have you yet been immortalised in sculpture?" Vizsla continues. "Perhaps in the classical

173

style, as a student of Euclid, or even as Pythagoras himself? You are of a similar reputation, I understand."

"You flatter me, Count, I am just a simple mathematician posing as an economist, currently a humble servant of the state."

"I have heard that today you bought most of Degas' collection. For such an irrepressible man, the purchase of two more by Monsieur Matisse will be yet another artistic and financial investment of the most secure and rewarding kind," Vizsla goes on. "Your friends will adore them, they will come to view them in the comfort of your Blueberry home."

"Bloomsbury," interjects Holmes.

Vizsla grimaces and tosses Holmes a nod of mock thanks.

"They are presently valued at a high price. I must charge clients of lesser intellect and judgement these sums because I myself paid too much for them just one month ago. The art *lover* within my heart seduced the art *dealer* of my mind and now there will be less honey on the table."

Vizsla's eyes visibly moisten as he shrugs in sad resignation and looks to Maynard for sympathy. To Holmes' amazement, he seems to have succeeded.

"But it is only men of our sensibility which will appreciate the importance of these works," he says. "We love them as if they were our own children and so I can offer this pair for just five hundreds of your pounds. My man will pack them for you now and they will speak most eloquently to your London friends of its owner's fine tastes."

"Maynard, we really should be getting back," says Holmes. "It is almost eleven."

Vizsla keeps smiling, watching his prey, the ends of his fingers now tapping together expectantly.

"Yes, you're quite right Holmes," says Maynard, Vizsla's spell suddenly broken. "Thank you Count, but we must leave. I will consider your generous offer and perhaps phone you tomorrow. In any event, I will certainly tell my London acquaintances of your collection here."

Vizsla's mouth tightens for a few seconds as if trying to conceal his anger at Holmes' untimely intervention then looks across at Leconte and resignedly gestures to him to lead the Englishmen back upstairs.

"Thank you, Lord Maynard, but please do not tell of this collection to the outsiders. The visit here is by private invitation and only at times which are convenient to my circumstances," says Vizsla, with a short bow.

The Count hangs back as they exit, switching off lights and locking doors behind them with small but audible sighs. Back upstairs, at the front door, the thanks and farewells are well-mannered but cool before Leconte announces that he will stay on for a while to "discuss another matter."

As the door closes and the two Englishmen walk back along the side of the main house, they strain to see into the shadows around them. All is still and there seems no threat nor danger but both now realise their drunken folly in undertaking such an expedition into the unknown.

"What do you think Leconte wanted to talk to Vizsla about?" Holmes asks in hushed tones.

"Money I should think," says Maynard. "He probably wants a commission for bringing us here. He'll be saying that it isn't his fault that nothing was bought."

"The Count is more than a salesman, he's a sorcerer," says Holmes. "I must confess, I thought you would buy those overpriced pictures. I am so greatly relieved that you saw sense in the end."

"I didn't!" says Maynard. "It was my own pecuniary limitations which stayed my hand. The money I'd allocated myself for this adventure was used up on Monsieur Cezanne's *Apples* earlier today. It was that alone which stopped me."

"You must hang it somewhere prominent to remind you of your near folly. It saved you from an ill-judged investment!" says Holmes, chuckling as they open the gate and go out onto the quiet boulevard, bathed in the light of the pale moon. "And I do not believe Cubism will ever amount to anything – it is no more than a fad. You had a lucky escape," he adds.

Maynard shrugs, believing Holmes to be mistaken. He smiles to himself as he looks up and down the Bois du Boulogne, half-expecting to see either Alice or her Doctor confederate peering out from behind a tree trunk or hedge, watching over them. But there is no sign of anyone. The avenue sleeps.

"I wonder why the Germans haven't bombed us tonight," muses Holmes as they stand looking out for a passing cab to take them back to the Crillon. "With our High Command in bickering disarray and the allied forces unable to even formulate a coherent plan let alone implement one, a strike at the capital now would be a mortal blow."

The mystery of the German non-action directed against Paris is solved the next morning at breakfast when Tyndale-Atkinson tells them that last night the enemy had bombed Abbeville, to the north. They are trying to cut Paris off from the rest of France and sever its supply lines. There were thirty-seven raids and most of the town and the railway station were still ablaze. Maynard and Holmes catch each other's eye but say nothing. Both know that Abbeville is on their route home. Tyndale-Atkinson says also that Monsieur Leconte has been reassigned to other duties.

17

An Embassy Lunch

Holmes' sleepless night is the result of too much wine and a late return from their nocturnal dealings with the Count and he wakes with a headache and feelings of foreboding. Throughout his ablutions and dressing, try as he might to silence the voices of disquietude, they whisper to him that his luck is about to run out. Tyndale-Atkinson's news at breakfast serves only to confirm that he has been tempting fate too long already and that soon, perhaps tonight on the journey home, the reaper's skeletal hands will wield the scythe and cut him down.

After breakfast, Maynard goes to his Inter Ally meeting and Holmes returns to his room to finish packing for their departure. They would leave after dinner this evening and take the 10.30 p.m. train. This assumes of course that both station and train still exist by then and that travel anywhere beyond the suburbs is even possible. Tyndale-Atkinson estimates that in the last three days, 500,000 panic-stricken Parisians have left their city. He says that the train termini serving the French west coast and the south –

Montparnasse and Gare de Lyon, have seen bullying men force aside families and the aged in order to secure the few remaining seats. At Saint-Lazare and Gare du Nord, the trains now are very scarce. The German net is closing fast.

By 10.00 a.m., Holmes is at Knoedlers gallery, organising tonight's transportation of the paintings. He finds that the day's first harbinger of bad luck is waiting for him as Hamann and Davey tell him that no boxes or trunks can be found in the whole of Paris. Their only hope lies in the great packing-case magnate of Paris, a Monsieur Malherbe, who was summoned more than an hour ago in order to broker a supply of transit crates. Holmes reflects on their good fortune in at least having Knoedlers at their side. It will be their contacts and reputation which will ensure that they get the best of attention even if no final solution is ultimately possible.

Malherbe arrives at eleven, a short, frock-coated man wearing a top hat and accompanied by two staunch-looking female assistants in blue blouses. The conversation which follows is for the most part in French but where the speed and subtlety of the words prompts a look of confusion on Holmes' face, Davey translates. As Malherbe explains the drought of containers in the city brought about by the mass exodus of citizens and businesses, there is much hand-waving, bowing and regret, but his final conclusion is predictable.

"Je regrette monsieur," says Malherbe, turning to Holmes, *"c'est impossible."*

"Then why take the considerable trouble to come here at all?"

"Pardon monsieur? Je ne comprends pas…"

Davey jumps quickly in, translating Holmes' words into a more polite form.

"Monsieur Holmes demande respectueusement s'il n'y a vraiment plus rien à faire?"

"En raison de mon respect pour Knoedler et la Grande-Bretagne, je pourrai peut-être jouer une dernière carte…" explains Malherbe, with the flicker of a smile playing at the corners of his mouth.

"Yes, of course," says Holmes, taking out his wallet and producing two-hundred francs in crisp banknotes. *"Nous aurons besoin d'une seule caisse d'environ deux cents sur trois cents de vos centimètres pour emporter une paire de peintures à l'huile encadrées d'ici au Gare du Nord avant 22 heures. ce soir."*

Malherbe's eyes flick down onto the wad of notes then back to Holmes. The Frenchman holds Holmes's gaze. Accepting the inevitable, Holmes produces another fifty franc note. He does not care to haggle. Malherbe proffers a nod of assent and takes the money.

"Yes, they will be at Gare du Nord by ten o'clock tonight. I will have to deprive one of my diplomat clients of their travelling crates in order to serve you but then, unlike Great Britain, they are only a small country," says Malherbe, now in perfect English. "So please, pass my card to your

Ambassador. We have not yet had the honour of contracting their business."

Holmes takes the man's card, shakes his hand and smiles thinly. They had both got what they wanted. Malherbe has sold a service to a stranger at four times its proper value, and Holmes has the satisfaction of knowing that the precious paintings would now be safely packaged. He has also rightly read another man's low character whose few grains of integrity can be bought for a handful of francs. As soon as Malherbe leaves the gallery, Holmes crumples the man's business card in his hand and tosses it into the nearest waste paper bin.

The rest of the morning is spent on the final details of their departure – on the transit documents and in organising the materials they will need to pack the remainder of the paintings. Waterproof paper, string, twine, nails, tacks and pincers, are all bought out from Knoedlers store rooms and set aside, ready for use once the auction is ended at six o'clock and the pictures are brought here from the Petit gallery. Satisfied he can do no more to prepare for their escape, Holmes, accompanied by Davey and Hamaan, sets-off for lunch at the British Embassy, there to meet with Maynard and Chamberlain, whose economic wrangles with the other allies will now, hopefully, be over for the day. As good fortune would have it, the Embassy is located just two hundred yards away, on the same street as Knoedlers, close to the Elysee Palace.

Once past the Embassy gates and the identity-checking British soldiers, they walk across an inner courtyard and up grand steps to a front door set under a wrought iron balcony supported by two pairs of Ionic columns. Maynard, Chamberlain and other members of the Inter Ally Council have only just arrived and are signing the visitors' book in the hallway as Holmes goes inside. His mouth almost falls open as he marvels at the sumptuous interior.

"I'd forgotten, this is your first visit here," says Maynard, seeing his friend's awe. "Let me take you on the shilling tour before we have lunch."

In typical manner, Maynard lectures and pontificates as they walk, his commentary as entertaining as it is well-informed. They stroll along the cool, white-marble floored corridors, peering into wondrous salons with silk damask wallpapers. The ballroom, the State Dining Room, the galleried library...

"It is described by some as the most precious architectural pearl in all of Paris and they do not exaggerate."

For the life of him, Holmes cannot see the difference between the Crillon hotel, which Maynard so despised, and this place, which he seems to adore. Perhaps it is that one is for commercial purpose and the other an instrument of diplomacy, that the hotel is faux and this authentic? Or are Maynard's architectural tastes simply more refined than his own?

"It was built in the 1720s as a Duke's palace then bought by Napoleon's sister, Pauline Borghese, in 1803. By then she was the wife of an Italian prince – the décor and the furniture is hers," Maynard says, stopping to point out an ornate monumental clock. "...many of her collections are still here."

"And yet it is now our Embassy?"

"Well it seems our Pauline was quite a girl...." confides Maynard.

Just as he is about to share what promises to be an amusing story of scandal and impropriety, lunch is called. As the Degas auction would start at three, they are both grateful it is not a long, drawn-out formal affair. After the arrival of the Ambassador, Sir Francis Bertie, and the playing of the National Anthem by a string quartet, lunch is a stand-up buffet, a *service à l'anglaise* with two dispensers of hot dishes, one at each end of a long table covered in cold selections of meats, fish, savoury pastries, vegetables and fruits. As they wait their turn at the table, Maynard quickly attracts a small crowd around him – well-to-do British businessmen and traders based in Paris, two junior diplomats and a young army officer. Maynard is known in these circles as an influential man whom it is good to get to know.

Once the group have their comestibles, the conversation moves swiftly from the work of the Inter-Ally Council, which that morning has clearly not gone well, onto the current parlous state of Paris' defences. To distract and lift the gloom and with his plate piled high with food and a glass of

183

champagne on the mantelpiece next to him, Maynard continues with his potted history of the embassy. As well as having Holmes' attention, he is now the focus of a small audience and is in his element.

"…and so by all accounts, with her husband out of the way, Pauline, the Emperor's sister, would hold the most debauched receptions, *levees* attended only by young men, where she would parade around in very few clothes so as to display her widely-admired wares. Unfortunately, what would follow is not recorded in reliable historical detail but the spirit of this place was obviously downright priapic…*un temple du phallus!*"

Even the normally starchy Holmes chuckles along as Maynard holds the crowd like a music hall entertainer.

"It is said she had a magnificent black man to carry her in and out of the bath…"

"I might get one of those for my wife!" says one of the English businessmen. The whole group whoop with delight.

"…and if Pauline felt the cold, she would warm her feet on the *décolletage* of a serving wench lying on the floor," says Maynard.

Holmes frowns a little, his French insufficient to make the translation. "The top of her titties," explains the young soldier with a guffaw. All roar

184

loudly causing the rest of the gathering to turn and stare. Undeterred by the room's disapproval, Maynard keeps going.

"But her brother Napoleon wasn't going to be left out of the bacchanalian fun and so came here regularly to fornicate with one of his sister's ladies-in-waiting. We think they would conjoin out there in the garden, their favourite bower being where the current ambassador and his wife now like to take tea!"

More hilarity ensues and the senior embassy staff are now frowning.

"And what became of Madame Borghese in the end?" asks Holmes in quieter tones, now trying to calm things.

"It's a sad tale, a veritable Greek Tragedy" replies Maynard, with mock pathos. His audience too don faux expressions of sadness. "Of course, Bonaparte was defeated and in 1814 his sister joined him on Elba. She sold this house and its entire contents to none other than the Duke of Wellington. Everything was included - lock, stock and beds. Even these Ormolu firedogs once belonged to her," he says, playfully kicking the edge of the ornamental coal basket in the fireplace hearth next to him.

"But gentlemen, that is not the end of it. Wellington agreed to pay her the sale price of £40,000 in instalments of gold which she then secretly passed to her brother Napoleon. His escape, return to power and the slaughter of seven thousand of our troops at Waterloo was financed by British gold! Sophocles himself could not have concocted so dark an irony."

Two men in the group wince a little, unsmiling. They are not sure if this is a suitable subject for mirth.

"And a hundred years later, we are still subsidizing the French state!" says the young soldier, obviously now a little the worse for lunchtime champagne.

"Now, now, that's not the spirit," replies Maynard in playful reproach. "Outside of these walls we are their guests and you sir, are, in effect, under the command of a French General."

"Indeed I am, but many now say that Haig gave ground too easily on that matter…"

"Poor Pauline died when she was only forty-four," says Maynard, cutting back in to prevent the youngster saying anything else he might regret. "A stomach tumour – brought on by the pox some say. But at least Wellington had the good grace to allow this house to remain as our embassy. It was, I dare say, more out of embarrassment than patriotism."

The party are laughing a little less now at what sounds suspiciously like subversive, socialist tendencies breaking cover. Making fun of the French was one thing but it was quite another to question the judgment and character of the Iron Duke, particularly in a time of war. Any further social awkwardness is, however, headed-off by the arrival of one of the ambassador's assistants.

"I am most sorry to interrupt gentlemen but could Sir Maynard and Mr Holmes please join the ambassador in his office? His Excellency understands you must soon depart and there are important matters he wishes to discuss."

Maynard and Holmes take their leave and the Ambassador's Secretary leads them back to the entrance hall, up a wide granite staircase and along a first floor corridor to a double-door decorated with gilt-framed rectangles containing acanthus leaf and lyre motifs. Inside is the greatest degree of ostentatiousness Holmes has ever seen in a single room. Every inch is dripping in French Empire excess – crystal chandeliers, gilded bronze-framed furniture, rich red velvet upholstery and curtains, walls covered in Corinthian pilasters and vertical panels surrounding monumental paintings. On the stuccoed ceiling are five large circular paintings showing scenes from antiquity of woodland nymphs and goddesses, one in each corner of the room and one directly above the central crystal chandelier. One half of the room is occupied by a large oval table with seating for eight, whilst next to the black marble fireplace a small circular table had been positioned between two comfortable looking basket chairs. Next to the window is a handsome writing desk and behind it sits the Ambassador, Baron Bertie of Thame. As they walk in, he finishes writing and stands up. The Secretary gestures to Holmes and Maynard to proceed, bows and retreats backwards out of the room, closing the double doors behind him.

"Welcome, both," says the Ambassador as he stands and extends a hand to his visitors. "Maynard, good to see you again, and Mr Holmes I presume? A pleasure to meet the esteemed Director of our National Gallery."

Francis Bertie is a plump man, well into his 70s and at first meeting, sharp-eyed, warm and likeable.

"Your Excellency", says Holmes. "Thank you so much for your kind invitation."

"No ceremony please, not behind closed doors anyway. Plain 'Bertie' will do nicely."

"The Ambassador enjoys its ambiguous nature – it being both a surname and Christian name," Maynard says, chipping in.

"Always have and always will...used it ever since I was a boy. And how go the negotiations of the Inter Ally Council, Maynard?"

"To be frank, sir, they are literally a French farce. The USA are holding fast to their terms regarding interest rates on our borrowings and insist on securing our remaining American investments as part of any future agreement."

Bertie shrugs, walks his two visitors across the room to the conference table and sits them down.

"I shall continue to put our case but under current circumstances I hold few cards in my hand," adds Maynard. "We have a war to win and need the money with which to do it."

"The Americans invented Poker and play it very well," says Bertie. "My view has always been that the European powers, including I might add our German cousins, should have stood together to fend off both the avaricious Americans and rampant Russians. Not that anyone in London ever listened to me and still do not. With respect, your Inter Ally Council is a Special Mission which bypasses the established lines of diplomacy. Esher's Military Mission is another which has led to much misunderstanding between ourselves and the French. I trust better the old school of established protocols and Court procedures. It has taken centuries for them to evolve and they exist in those forms for good reason."

"I hope I'm not being presumptuous in saying that our relationship with the French, your sponsorship of the *Entente Cordial*, shows the effectiveness of such an approach," says Holmes.

"I am grateful for your compliment, Mr Holmes, but I only strengthened what Lord Lansdowne and Cambon had already built before me. Now I fear I will be remembered as the Ambassador who had to flee from an invasion of Paris."

"Nonsense," says Maynard. "We shall prevail. The mood here today is one of great optimism."

Bertie smiles at Maynard as if to say 'I know you are lying to make me feel better,' then winces a little.

"How are you Bertie? You are still pained at times I see."

"I am much improved, thank you. They think I have the beginnings of the condition which did for the much-maligned Pauline," says the ambassador turning to Holmes. "It does however not arise from the same cause I assure you!"

Holmes smiles gently at the old man, for the first time noticing the age lines on his face and the tiredness in his small, ice-blue eyes.

"I believe I overheard you entertaining our guests with accounts of the poor woman's tenure here?" says Bertie turning to Maynard.

Holmes notices that although Bertie is smiling he was clearly not much amused by Maynard's apparent lack of compassion for a soul who had so clearly lost her way.

"…but did you know that her protection during the carnage of colonial Saint-Dominque was provided by none other than Monsieur Jacques de Norvin, the very same man I believe you two pirates have now got a portrait of?"

Neither man answers. Bertie is making the point that though clever, Maynard does not know nor understand everything. At the very moment Holmes is struck by the up-to-date accuracy of Bertie's intelligence, the Ambassador sees what he is thinking and immediately responds.

"Come now, Mr Holmes, you are not surprised by my knowing what goes on in my own city?"

Before Holmes can answer, Bertie has fixed his eyes back on Maynard.

"And I'll wager you didn't know that our young Mr Churchill was conceived under this roof or that your friend Somerset-Maugham was born within these very walls."

"You're right, I didn't. But Willie's not exactly a friend."

"But he's one of your lot I think?"

A pause hangs heavy in the air.

"I mean that he is an intellectual, an aesthete," says the Ambassador, finally breaking the awkward silence.

Maynard doesn't answer.

"Maugham's father was a lawyer in Paris and not wanting their son to be born French, made sure the birth took place here at the embassy. Back then, the French government were about to introduce a new law stating that anyone who was born on French soil would automatically be French and therefore eligible for conscription to serve in the expected war of revenge against the Prussians. But the army got your friend in the end. From 1914 he was here in France fighting, well, ambulance driving anyway, but not for the French, for us! You can't change what you're destined to be, eh Maynard?!"

Maynard remains impassive, all too aware of the Ambassador's unsubtle sleight. But he has a soft spot for old buffers like Bertie. Like many from the lower tiers of the English aristocracy, he is affable and intelligent but made foolish and bigoted by the brutalising world of public schools and class prejudice. And as with many such men, he is beset by personal weakness and unhappiness.

"Maugham's with the SIS now I think, one of our spy chaps…anyway, time is pressing on. To business," says Bertie, going across to his desk to retrieve a small leather portfolio. He returns, sits down at the table and opens the wallet to reveal a tiny ledger and two cheque books. Writing the date and a signature completed with an extravagant flourish of the wrist, he hands a blank cheque to Holmes.

"Once you've completed your buyings at the auction rooms, fill-in the amount and give this to their accountant. Galerie Petit already know the monies are coming so no questions will be asked. Oh, and Austen Chamberlain will have to counter-sign of course."

"Of course," says Maynard, reaching across to take charge of the cheque, "but this is for External Government Expenditure for which *I'm* responsible. Thank you for facilitating our dealings Ambassador, we are most grateful."

"I don't suppose there's enough of your External Government Expenditure left over to buy my lovely old writing desk here?" he says, turning to point at his inlaid *escritoire*. "I fear the Germans will steal it away or destroy it out of spite. £1200 would suffice…"

Holmes looks over at the desk and believing Bertie to be joking, is about to laugh along. But neither Maynard nor the Ambassador are smiling. It suddenly occurs to him that Bertie might be in some sort of financial difficulty brought about by who knows what – gambling, failing family estates at home, bad investments, bad women…

"I'm afraid not old chap, you'll just have to hope that we win."

The ambassador shrugs. "Then I'll phone my secretary to show you out. Good luck with your more easily justifiable purchases" he says as he looks unhappily away then stands up and returns to his desk.

As Bertie stares out of the window, speaking on the phone, and the two friends stand up to leave, Holmes casually looks at a small framed photograph sitting on a nearby shelf. It shows two liveried footmen clinging to the back of the Ambassador's carriage, taken here, outside in the courtyard of the embassy. For some unaccountable reason, he turns the frame over and is shocked to find that on the back is a grainy photo of two naked women, dancers or prostitutes he presumes, in intimate embrace. He hastily repositions it but notices that the signature on the front is Eugene Pirou's, celebrity photographer and artist. He knows that Pirou was the maker of an infamous piece of early erotic cinema, *Le Coucher de la Mariee*. Holmes remembers that the pornographers were quick to seize the opportunities provided by the new medium, for 'Bedtime for the Bride' was made in 1896, less than a year after the first public screening of a projected film. He wonders if Bertie has seen it.

18

Mixed Fortunes

They walk back across town through the still empty, nervous streets, along du Faubourg Saint-Honoré, the Boulevard de la Madeleine and the Rue de Seze, to the Galerie Petit. As there has been no shelling for the past twenty hours, the sale room is once again filled to bursting and it is not long after the auction begins that they realise prices have re-inflated and that today the going will not be to their advantage. Holmes bags a set of Gavani lithographs and paintings by Fourain, Delacroix, Ricard and Rousseau but their most sought-after works, those identified by Nessa and Duncan in particular, elude them. The El Greco, a Perronneau and more Gauguins are secured by other buyers.

Holmes is pleased with some purchases, lukewarm to most and downright disappointed with the rest. Today, their position in the room is far from the easel and he has bought one or two pieces almost by mistake. But no matter, he tells himself, yesterday they secured most all they wanted at prices he could not have dreamed of and he still has five thousand pounds remaining of their Special Grant. For one horrible moment he worries that Maynard and Chamberlain may try to recover the unspent monies but neither have said anything about it. He hopes they will remain silent on the matter and that Chamberlain is perhaps even countenancing another such venture to future auctions. He understands there is still much of the Degas collection left unsold. When the time is right, he will press him once again on the possibility.

When the sale is over, the five men remain seated, waiting in silence to be called through to pay for and collect the spoils of their past two days' labours. It is almost six o'clock when their turn finally comes. Holmes looks nervously at his pocket watch. Their train leaves Gare du Nord at ten-thirty and there is still much left to do. As Chamberlain signs the cheques at the cashier's table, Holmes can see into the storerooms beyond as his purchases are clothed in loose protective covers and got ready for carriage to Knoedlers where they will receive their final preparation for the journey back to England.

Thirty minutes later, some carried by Maynard, Holmes, Davey and Hamann, others by helping hands from Galerie Petit, the art works arrive at Knoedlers and are joyously welcomed inside by the office staff. Chamberlain has departed for the Crillon having urged them to be quick in their work and soon all have removed their jackets and are on their hands and knees on a cleared floor, wrapping the art in the heavy, brown, weather-proof paper and where possible, covering the packages in thin skins of protective plywood. The dining-table sized Manet and the Delacroix take a full hour to wrap and it soon becomes clear that there will be neither the time now nor space on the train to package all the art in this manner. The call goes around the room to cease work. Holmes has another idea.

"Take the rest out of their frames and arrange them into bundles of five. We will stack or roll them up," he says, earmarking a half dozen as starters. "…but wrap all loosely. The thicker oils we shall keep flat, two sheets of paper between each with single-ply board on the outside, the portfolios too. The drawings and pastels can be rolled and we'll secure with string and wire. Each of us will take on a single part of the process, as in one of Mr Ford's factories," says Holmes, jollying everyone along. Hamann, Davey and Maynard look concerned.

"The works will be quite safe I assure you. I served as a printer-publisher for five years and know how to both package and move art."

"But none of your stock was of this delicacy and value surely?" says Maynard, dabbing his forehead with a handkerchief.

"All were worth money of the folding sort," replies Holmes, brushing aside Maynard's nervousness. "And we must ensure that they are easily portable. There will be few hired hands to help us at Gare du Nord I fear and even fewer at Boulogne. We may have to carry many ourselves and so we shall add holding handles and harnesses."

As they are small-sized, Maynard's four paintings can stay in their frames but even so, each requires careful attention and are sandwiched between stiff card, wrapped in thick brown paper and tied with wire. With some rearrangement of his belongings, they will fit into a suitcase.

Even with Holmes' new production line in place, the work takes longer than anticipated and by nine o'clock, they are only then packaging up the last of the works. As they finally finish to great relief, men in blue overalls from Malherbe's removal company arrive with the vast crate for the Manet and the Delacroix. In the downstairs lobby, just inside the front door, a red-faced, anxious Holmes greets them and asks for reassurance that they will get the art to the station in all haste so as to catch their ten-thirty train.

"À la gare du Nord dans une heure, à dix heures, dans exactement une heure, ils ne peuvent pas être en retard, le train n'attendra pas, ils n'ont qu'une heure!"

The foreman seems like an experienced man, well-used to fretting clients and he calms Holmes with a skilled nonchalance.

"Bien sûr qu'ils seront là monsieur, pourquoi ne le seraient-ils pas?" he says with an 'all will be well' shrug as he turns to his men with the instructions of commencement.

There is nothing more the Englishmen can do now except thank Hamann and Davey, tell them that a generous cheque awaits them at the British

Embassy, and walk back to the Crillon in the dark. But as they approach the hotel, they see that the entrance is now guarded by uniformed, armed gendarmes and soldiers, four of each. None of these sentinels smile or speak as they stand there, weapons drawn, scrutinising anyone who gets within ten feet of them. Even the few passers-by who scuttle home at the end of their working day are eyed with suspicion. Maynard realises they are not there to provide protection from insurgent Germans or saboteurs but from other Parisians, fellow Frenchmen bent on disorder or worse. The presence of these peace-keepers signals Government fears that lawlessness will erupt at the approach of the invading German army, that there will be power-grabs by the political classes, robbery and kidnap by the criminal class, and murderous retribution by Paris' underclass for crimes against its dispossessed. If Bolshevik rabble-rousers can rise-up in Russia why not here? Maynard reminds himself to take a care. This is no game, no Friday evening debating society. This is real.

Holmes and Maynard show their passports and room keys to the police and go into the empty foyer. No phones ring. The lifts are silent. The front desk is unmanned. Behind it, inside the Manager's Office, Maynard can see a man through a glass vision panel in the closed door. He is reading what seems to be a telegram and when he sees Maynard watching him, he pulls down the blind.

The Englishmen go up to their rooms and collect the last of their belongings and when they arrive back in reception, they find Chamberlain, Cravath, Mr Berry and the other delegates alongside two Mission secretaries and Nurse Alice. Everyone exchanges nervous greetings before Berry informs the party that the British Embassy has sent cars to take them to Gare du Nord station. There are no cabs to be had. They wait inside until five black limousines pull up in front of the Crillon then walk quickly out onto the pavement and climb in. Chamberlain, Berry, Holmes and Maynard share the same car. Maynard notices that Alice remains rear-guarding the final group until all are loaded. She is the last to step to safety.

When they arrive at the station, Berry acts as convener and, shouting above the hubbub, reminds them that the International Mission has reserved carriage Number 8 on the 10.30 train to Boulogne, leaving from platform 13. All should now make their way there as they have just thirty minutes in which to board. As the others move off, Berry takes Maynard and Holmes to one side and suggests they go to the luggage clerk's office to ensure that their precious cargo of art has arrived and is being loaded onto the train.

Inside the Gare du Nord, it is only the presence of many soldiers and police which controls the anxiety now threatening to engulf the place. Although most Parisians will flee west or south, perhaps five thousand are, like them, journeying north, towards the Channel ports or to connecting trains towards Brittany. Despite the wads of francs being waved under station staff noses and at ticket windows, Maynard sees that even the privileged-wealthy are being prevented from getting their own way. Many well-dressed gentlemen stand despondent – children, luggage and servants in tow. Some are English families, desperate to return home in case the whole of France falls. Among the crowd, arguments flare up into fist fights over access to trains, a place in a queue, and even the use of a luggage trolley. Under threat of arrest, disputes are forcefully quelled by the police. A loud vehicle backfire brings silence to the throng as they fear the monster gun has recommenced its deadly work. Panic momentarily freezes the action. A single shell landing here, now, would mean a hundred deaths, by fire and stampede as well as by white-hot razor-sharp shrapnel. But within five seconds, the hubbub begins again with renewed urgency.

Berry, Maynard and Holmes push through the tumult, find the luggage office and waving their passports and diplomatic passes, are allowed into the cavernous room, a haven of quiet order. Behind a long counter they see the personal luggage of the seventeen members of the International Mission including their own, being moved by porters from a neat pile in the corner out onto the platforms towards the trains. The packages of art are there too, being handled with dutiful care. All is well. The three men look at each other and exchange sighs as they stand relieved, watching the last of the bags and bundles of paintings disappear out through the door. But as it closes, job seemingly done, Holmes points a quivering finger at the seven by ten-foot crate containing the Delacroix and the Manet. It stands untouched, leaning against a back wall.

He walks quickly up to the desk and a uniformed clerk, his face hitherto buried deep in a large ledger, looks up with a blank expression. The man says nothing, waiting for Holmes to speak.

"Pardon monsieur, mais la valise fait partie de nos bagages et doit rejoindre les autres dans notre train pour Boulogne," says Holmes pointing at the monster case.

The short-statured official doesn't reply, instead picking up a leaflet of Regulations from the shelf beside him which he then slides across the counter. He adjusts his half-moon glasses then returns to his book-keeping, explaining the rules without looking up.

"Tous les colis d'une taille supérieure à deux cents centimètres de longueur ne peuvent pas être inclus dans les bagages personnels." he mutters, pointing at the text. Holmes turns to Maynard and Berry in desperation. He cannot follow what the silly little man is saying.

"He says that packages greater than two-hundred centimetres in length cannot be included as personal luggage," explains Maynard.

Holmes stares down at the paper but is struggling to understand its formal language, written as it is in a hybrid of post office jargon and legalise. The English equivalent would be hard enough to decipher but in French, it is quite beyond him. He looks again to his fellow countrymen for help and Berry moves to the counter. The clerk continues to write into his ledger.

"Je suis désolé d'insister, mais le contenu de cette affaire est d'importance internationale et fait partie de notre mission diplomatique ici, une mission qui a été demandée par votre propre gouvernement. Pourriez-vous s'il vous plaît organiser le chargement de la valise dans le train ? Il doit partir dans quinze minutes," says Berry. He is calm but

deadly firm. The clerk however, even in the face of such intimidation, remains utterly indifferent, continuing to attend to his work.

"Si vous ne nous aidez pas, Monsieur, je prendrai votre nom et signalerai votre obstruction au Premier ministre français lui-même. C'est une affaire internationale en temps de guerre!" threatens Berry, but still to no effect.

Maynard has been watching proceedings with growing amusement. The clerk with his stuck-down brilliantined hair, pale bookkeepers' face and pencil-line moustache, momentarily twisted his lips upon hearing Berry's threat but remained intransigent, continuing as before. His pursed, tight mouth put Maynard in mind of a particularly unattractive anus and he is still gently chuckling as he pushes past his friends to intervene.

"Excuse me gentlemen," he says. "Please allow me to resolve this little impasse."

Maynard speed-reads the postmaster's rules then, with a small smile of satisfaction, most politely addresses him.

"Alors monsieur, si nous faisons peser notre grande bête et vous payons le montant qu'elle dépasse la franchise pour 'bagage personnel', vous la passerez et la laisserez partir?"

"Oui monsieur, c'est exact," says the clerk. A twitch of amusement plays at the corners of his eyes as he looks at Maynard.

"Alors nous vous demandons de bien vouloir le faire," says Maynard.

The clerk nods respectfully, turns round and gives the necessary instructions to his two assistants then begins to make out the appropriate docket and luggage passes pulled from folders beneath his counter.

"It would seem that if we have our great beast weighed-in and pay for the amount it exceeds the allowance for 'personal luggage', they will pass it and allow it on its way," explains Maynard.

"Why didn't he say that before," exclaims an exasperated Holmes.
"Because you didn't ask him," Maynard whispers, signalling to his friend to keep his voice down.
"The rules say that if items of personal luggage exceed the maximum allowable size then an excess must be paid. If a passenger believes their belonging to be too large, they should request both its re-measurement and weighing before paying the additional tariff. You did not do this."

Holmes and Berry look incredulous but Maynard gestures to his friends, inviting them to look around the room. He is saying 'behold the little clerk's empire, here he is king.'
Maynard nods as his friends grasp this reality. To him this is well-trodden ground. He must charm, persuade, cajole and outwit bureaucrats, functionaries and paper-pushers, great and small, every day of his working week. And this isn't England where deference has down the centuries been

transfused into the blood of the lower orders, this is France. They had a revolution here. Citizens have their pride because each of them are *Ressortissants* – 'The French Nation', and all are equal and free, *les gens du grand collectif.*

Uniformed porters heave the great crate onto a weighbridge in the corner and shout out its load in kilos. The clerk purses his lips once again as he calculates the amount and fills out a ticket which he passes to Maynard. The excess weight charge for this now officially declared piece of 'personal luggage of one of the seventeen members of the International Mission' comes to the princely sum of 10 centimes. Holmes and Maynard smile at each other in amused disbelief and then watch as their cargo is duly taken to the train. All three Englishmen thank the clerk and follow the porters out through the door. The little official returns their thanks and bids them *bon voyage.* Judging by his smirk of contentment, the episode has made his day.

On the other side of the station, they board the eight-coached, overcrowded train as it puffs restlessly at its platform and just five minutes later, they leave Paris to its fate. Now they will travel to the north to meet theirs, whatever it may be.

19

Amid the Chaos

In Sanctuary Wood, Ypres Sector, March 1918. Adrian Hill.

Just as Berry had promised, the International Mission is allocated a long carriage to itself. At one end are enough couchettes, bunks and sleeping compartments for the entire party to each have a bed for the night. The rear half of their car is fitted with upholstered bench seats, tables and chairs in the form of a dining salon and, as luck would have it, is immediately adjacent to the baggage car and their precious cargo of art. Their carriage also has its own small kitchen, bar, Water Closets and wash basins, and so its passengers need have no contact with other travellers. Maynard notices that their trooper guardians are no longer with them, reassigned to other more pressing duties just as General Sykes had warned. The doctor too is gone. Only a single soldier has been left with them along with their nurse-spy Alice. He hopes neither will be needed.

Within an hour, the frayed suburban edges of the city now far behind them, the mission's exhausted envoys and staff are tucked-up in their couchettes, asleep. Only Maynard remains dressed and awake, sitting in the dining car reading through the draft Inter-Ally agreements, formulated at this morning's meeting. He shakes his head and mutters as he scans the text. There is still much cursed muddle and ambiguity to be resolved – by Monday next, he will need a coherent, workable plan for the management of the American loans, prepared in sufficient detail to be presented to the Chancellor. But it is too late-night now to do more. His mind is become heavy, sluggish – full of the toxic residue of the day's tribulations.

At eleven-thirty, just as he is about to retire and the tiny bar and kitchen shortly to close, Nurse Alice appears. Even dressed in her Ward Sister's uniform and clearly exhausted, to Maynard she still has something of the gypsy dancer about her. She asks for a brandy nightcap from the bar steward who steals a glance at her, intrigued, as he pours out the *Armagnac*. This breaking of social convention, a woman entering a bar alone, even on a train, troubles her not one jot. Maynard studies her again and decides she is a well-practised sole practitioner, a Luna wolf, moving at will through a man's world, her current mission her only real concern. The barman, initially taken aback by her calm assurance as she spoke in accent-free French to him, looks as if he now accepts that for her, the usual etiquettes and expectations of female subservience do not apply. They briefly exchange pleasantries, mistress and manservant small talk, before she turns and raises her glass in Maynard's direction. He presumes she is toasting his auction success.

He bundles up his papers and walks over to the bar to ask if he may join her for this last drink of the day. She invites him to sit with her as the barman locks up, says goodnight and leaves the salon, closing the door behind him. Now they are alone in the soft-lit carriage with only the click-clack of the train to accompany their quiet assignation.

"So, triumph complete Mr Keynes? – Frogs outplayed, Huns evaded. All we have to do now is to get you and your art safe home."

Maynard acknowledges her congratulations with a smile and a curt nod. "And we are all most grateful for your good stewardship of our mission. I am sorry if we, I, made difficulties for you at times. Did your Nurse Taylor turn up?" he says, in concerned tones.

"No," she says impassively, sipping her brandy.

"What was his first name?"

"Daniel…'Danny'," she says.

She gives Maynard a cool stare and he can see that she cannot, will not, discuss the matter further. It probably did not end well. He wonders if she blames him for whatever became of her friend. He does. He leans across and lights her cigarette then watches her inhale the sweet smoke.

"Your 'nursing duties' shall we call them, are most hazardous are they not?"

Alice says nothing, only raising her eyebrows in a self-deprecating 'I suppose so' kind of a way.

"I find myself wondering why a lovely young woman would choose such a path?"

"It chose me. Besides, we're in a war and all must do their duty, give of their best in the ways they are most able to provide."

He smiles at her. It is almost as if she had overheard his previous conversation with Holmes, their exchange on the cross-channel voyage, and is now using his words to answer his own question.

"I'm no heroine," she goes on. "I didn't beat on their door, begging to let me in. I didn't even lean against it. I was just standing there when it fell open. I accepted the invitation to go inside."

Maynard draws on his cigar and waits for her to continue. She will tell him her story tonight he thinks. For just as we all must eventually confess – reveal and confide in others in the hope of receiving understanding, comfort and absolution, she will now invite another soul to share her weird little world for a short while. Maynard is lucky, he has trusted friends to whom he can unburden but this fighting queen, an Amazon warrior out there on the edge, can afford no such confessors. She holds his gaze for a second and he understands. The bargain will be that her story will never be revealed, even after the war is over, that the soldier's oath of allegiance is a tryst between them and the cause they serve and its secrets must be kept.

"I was nursing a wounded officer at General Hospital No 1 at Étretat near Le Havre in 1916," she says. "There were men of all nationalities and he overheard me speaking French, Flemish and German. We became friends. I told him I'd learnt languages through my father's Embassy postings, and that I could ride and swim…and shoot."

"And nurses and doctors are astute readers of the disposition, character and honesty of men," says Maynard. "You had the ideal qualities so he recommended you to his superiors back in London?"

Alice nods and takes another sip of brandy.

"I only realised he'd been interviewing me when the Matron asked if special duties might interest me. That if I wanted to do such work, I would be returning home for a while. A month later, I heard my officer friend had died."

Alice pauses for a moment and puts out her cigarette. "And now, well…here I am."

"I know there are many women working in such a fashion here in France and in occupied Belgium and Holland too. Cumming told me they are called *La Dame Blanche*. They are Nurses like you, Medical Orderlies, and Midwifes whose jobs allow them to cross military lines carrying reports, some wrapped around the whale bones of their corsets!"

Alice puts a shushing forefinger to her smiling lips. She says nothing back to him but doesn't disagree.

"But saving stranded soldiers, reporting troop movements and the like puts such women at great risk?"

"Many have been arrested. My friend Aurelie was raped by German soldiers in punishment for suspected crimes, Louise de Bettignies is serving forced labour, Marie Vanhoutte imprisoned in '15, Gabrielle Petit and Edith Cavell are executed…" she says.

The silence between them is broken by a jolt to the carriage as the train brakes to a sudden standstill.

"I didn't know. You soldiers spare us Civil Servants much sad detail," says Maynard. "So having served your cause bravely for two long years, is it not time now to stop? You have already done more than any of our countrymen could reasonably expect."

"These are not reasonable times," she says, walking over to the window and gingerly lifting the blind. "You should sleep now. There is still far to go and need your wits about you tomorrow to get yourself and your treasure across the Channel. It will not be an easy crossing I'm afraid, the weather is forecast to be bad."

"You are right, of course. Thank you," says Maynard, before asking one last question. "By the way, did you notice a tall man, dressed as a station guard, jump aboard our train in Boulogne when we first arrived?"

211

"Yes, why?" says Alice, still looking out of the train window as it lurches forward, continuing its onward journey.

"No particular reason, just idle curiosity."

"You're a bad liar, Mr Keynes," she says, turning to him with a girlish grin. "He stayed with us until Gare du Nord then disappeared into the crowds. Whoever he was working for I'll wager it wasn't the French railways."

"And is he here now, on-board?"

"It's on my list of things to do in the morning. I'll walk the train to check if he's there and we'll see if any other passengers look, how shall I put it, 'out of place'."

Maynard feels suddenly fearful for her and walks forward to put his arms gently around her.

"You will of course act with the utmost care," he says.

She squeezes him with a gentle reassurance then kisses him lightly on the cheek.

"Don't worry, this isn't the stuff of which heroines are made," she says, playfully tugging at her collar. "When the war is over I plan to have a long and happy life back in England, with many grandchildren to follow."

Maynard smiles and takes her hand.

"Then goodnight, Nurse Alice."

Both leave the bar, Maynard going to his couchette alone, Alice to disappear into the public train carriage beyond, her purpose unclear. They share one last look before she is gone.

The next morning, Holmes wakes at seven o'clock to silence, the train stopped in a station. They have made good progress overnight and are at what remains of Amiens. Over half-way now, it is just eighty miles to Boulogne. Holmes rises from his couchette and lifts the blind. He looks out at the deserted town, opens the compartment window and can just make out the sound of distant guns. But against all expectations, the booms are less than when they passed through here before. Then the peace is suddenly shattered. On an adjacent track, heading south, a locomotive speeds past with carriages and trucks full of men, stores and cannon. Two minutes later, another follows, and then another. It is an endless procession, heading towards the Front.

He hurries to the small WC to rescue his only tie from the wash basin then as he returns to his berth is met by an unperturbed Mr Berry bearing a breakfast consisting of bread roll, a stick of chocolate and half a tumbler of Sauterne, all presented on a piece of greasy brown paper. Holmes thanks him and deposits the feast on his bunk.

"Please," says Berry, "may I have the paper back? It's Mr Chamberlain's table cloth."

Austen is quite welcome to the disgusting sheet, Holmes thinks, it will surely stain and contaminate rather than protect. But for some it seems that a table cloth is a necessity no matter what its condition.

In the salon, Maynard waits in vain for Alice to appear. He has been up since six and has not breakfasted, drinking only thick sweet coffee from the time the waiter arrived on duty until now. At six-thirty, he ventured out into the rest of the train, went through the nearest carriages full of stale-smelling, *Gitanes*-smoking French, clambering over their luggage and children before being beaten back by the precarious effort of it all. Unless Alice has jumped-train, she is somewhere further forward carrying out reconnaissance, trailing their adversaries, doing battle. He fears she has moved beyond reach now, too distant from any meagre help he might provide.

The door opens and the voices of two men stir him from his reflections. Their sole trooper guard and a bedraggled young British officer walk in and go to the bar and ask for tea. The waiter is unsure of the appropriateness but when Maynard nods his acquiescence, the men are served. He stands up and joins them, fast learning that this lieutenant has become separated from his unit and will now ride the train north for a few miles in order to rendezvous with his comrades. Maynard urges him to recount his tale as their trooper salutes and returns to his guard duties at the end of the carriage. The lad begins his story but frequently stumbles in the retelling, barely making eye contact.

"We were told to evacuate at speed but the enemy were well in our rear, in possession of Lamotte....the bombardment was of great weight and ferocity. Our section included four lads who had just turned eighteen – they'd only arrived two weeks ago and the barrage was their first experience of shell fire. One kept calling 'mother'. Such a hell makes weaklings of the strongest. No human was made to stand such torture and mental anguish. Then their trench was blown in and we never saw them again."

The lieutenant gulps down his water and half of his coffee then continues.

"We waited at Coyeux but were then counter-attacked and our acting Commanding Officer wounded. We had to fight rear-guard actions along the riverbed. I was told to leave with the wounded, westwards, to protect the ambulances you see…"

Maynard obtains more coffee and a large pitcher of water to rehydrate the man's disturbed body chemistries.

"The Germans attacked from the north, east and north-west around Rosières. They are now but nine miles from here – you are in grave jeopardy," he says nervously, before regaining his composure. "We abandoned Bray and the line of the Somme, and the bridgeheads westwards towards Sailly-le-Sec. Montdidier and its comm's centre was lost by the French on the 27th. That was…yesterday…I think, yes…I'm sure it was. Yesterday. Twenty-nine Hun divisions attacked the Third Army and were repulsed. German troops advanced against the Fifth, from the original front at St. Quentin, penetrated 40 miles and reached Montdidier. Rawlinson replaced Gough, who was 'Stellenbosched.'"

Maynard does not know this term and frowns.

"Dismissed, sacked!" says the lieutenant, catching Maynard's look of confusion. "It was damn rum if you ask me. He organised a most successful retreat, given the conditions. They had no proper cause to do that…"

Chamberlain, Fry, Booth and Buckmaster enter the salon and the young officer quickly stands up, gives his thanks to Maynard and takes his leave. He says he will sit in the guard's van until they reach Abbeville. Short of rendering the lad unconscious or kidnapping him, Maynard can do nothing

215

to prevent the lieutenant's return to the front. He is without any doubt unfit for his duties but that will not stop him from fulfilling them, not until he is either maimed or killed.

The boy closes the door behind him and as Maynard remains seated, powerless to help further, Chamberlain announces that he wishes to see the art one last time before they reach Boulogne.
"…just in case we're hit and lose the bloody lot!"
Holmes and Chamberlain walk through the carriage to the baggage car, ask the attendant to unlock the cages then inspect the paintings they can see. Only a few are viewable by carefully folding back the edges of their wrappings but nonetheless Chamberlain seems pleased as he surveys the haul. Maynard joins them, trying to put to one side the young lieutenant's grim story and his thoughts of concern.

"This is very well done, Charles! Again, my congratulations, and to you too Maynard – the mastermind. We have our very own Holmes and Moriarty, do we not!"

All three men smile and look proudly on the swag of their labours.
"I wonder what Baron Schwiter or Monsieur Norvin would have said if you'd told them about their future adventures – their likenesses being transported across a battlefield and carried off as booty!" conjectures Chamberlain.

"Norvin would have been accepting and probably much amused," says Holmes. "He was after all, a man of war himself, a soldier of fortune. Schwiter would have been less philosophical I think. As well as being an artist, he had many Old Masters. He would have disapproved of Degas' collection being broken up and cast to the four winds."

"Ever the curator, eh Holmes!" Maynard says. "The Baron's fine portrait will now be seen by hundreds of thousands, perhaps by millions, until the end of time. We have saved him from a life spent in the dull obscurity of a private collection in Berlin or from a burning building in Paris."

Holmes smiles and nods, gratefully accepting Maynard's reassurances. "We will now leave you in peace, my children," Holmes says to the art, casting his eyes one last time around their booty. "We shall see you again on the Boulogne dockside before carrying you across the sea to your new home."

The three confederates leave the paintings to themselves and to the care of the Baggage Car attendant. Maynard is sure the man speaks no English as judging by his still sleepy manner, he can have no idea of the monetary worth of the crates and packages in his charge today.

The train moves out of Amiens, trundles along at a steady speed and within an hour, they have rolled once more into Abbeville. Palls of smoke still rise from the town and Maynard can see that most of the buildings are shattered. As they approach the miraculously still intact long, low, redbrick station, Maynard can see that the surrounding goods yards and warehouses have also been reduced to smouldering rubble. The streets are empty of both civilians and Allied soldiers. The train judders to a halt and Maynard sits in the Salon and watches the young Lieutenant disembark. The lad stares around him then slings his rifle over his shoulder and walks towards the *sortie* sign. As he disappears from sight, Maynard thinks again of Alice and recalls part of a poem by Edmund Haraucourt, a *Rondel de l'Adieu*

'To say goodbye, is to die a little'.

20

Once More into Boulogne

Dazzle Leave Ships, Boulogne. Charles Bryant.

The train is held stopped in Abbeville station without explanation. Five minutes becomes fifteen and then thirty. An impatient Maynard spots a scurrying porter, enquires as to the cause and is told it's the train's own footplate crew, the driver and fireman, not the signalmen, who are responsible for the hold-up. They are demanding reassurances on the condition of the track ahead and workings of the points on the edge of town, both of which were damaged in the bombing raids of two nights ago. Maynard is told this could take some time. As the porter turns to walk away, he warns that all should remain on board, it is thought too dangerous to venture out onto the platforms. Snipers may have already infiltrated the town's now undermanned defences. It is not safe to break cover. Maynard conveys the news to those gathered in the salon and as they listen to his report, their hitherto convivial chatter subsides into nervous silence. On the approaches to the town, it was clear that Allied gun emplacements had been abandoned. They know too that most of their troops have been moved east and south to fight the German advance and that there is now no air cover. If the packed train's position is reported by enemy reconnaissance or local spies, they are fish in a barrel. Maynard finishes delivering his unwelcome news and returns to his seat.

Time is slowed, the seconds drag past. Half-hearted conversations begin then falter and stall. Some close their eyes in mock sleep whilst others read. Chamberlain watches the skies as he taps his fingers on the table. Holmes cannot rid his mind of van Eyck's painting of a sacrificial lamb tethered to an altar and Booth constantly examines his watch and wipes the sweat from his brow. The air inside the carriage becomes stuffy and even the unflappable Berry loosens his collar stud. As they approach the hour mark, Lord Buckmaster allows an involuntary 'Oh, for God's sake…" to escape under his breath. He shakes his head in self-reproach then silently looks down at the table. In the far distance, three shells explode one after the other and transmit faint but unmistakable vibrations through the carriage. No-one moves a muscle. The explosions cease but for how long, Maynard wonders. Perhaps those same guns are now being trained on them?

He has begun to play an amusing parlour game with himself, speculating on who will crack next and what form their loss of nerve will take. Will it be Chamberlain? – no, he is like a rock. Might Berry finally uncoil and embarrass himself? Holmes remains at-risk... But before Maynard can complete his shortlist and allocate suitable odds of probability, the train jolts forward and inches its way out of the station. Everyone waits until they are clear of the Abbeville signal box before collectively exhaling their bated breath, followed by measured 'hurrahs' and ripples of relieved laughter. Buckmaster gets up and hurries to the WC. Maynard supposes that fear and the unexpected lurch of the train has caused an uncontrollable body malfunction, which, under the circumstances, is quite understandable.

Around noon, the moody sky darkens and rain starts to fall, making diagonal rivulets across the windows and obscuring Maynard's view out. A few miles beyond Abbeville, at Noyelles-sur-Mer, where the railway line turns northwards to run parallel to the Channel coast, he supposes he sees the flash of canon fire on the inland horizon but cannot be sure. There's just forty-five miles to go now and he knows that once they cross the River Somme, the run-in to Boulogne should be straightforward – as much as any journey can be, here, now, in these desperate hours. All will be well unless of course the Germans have broken through and cut-off their escape. Then what, he wonders? – a race west to the ports of Dieppe or Le Havre with a baggage car full of art treasures and the German army in pursuit? But if it comes to it, then somehow they will pull it off, *he* will pull it off, and the adventure will be even more astounding and more worthy of re-telling. Sitting opposite him, Stanley Buckmaster, Liberal MP and former Lord Chancellor of England, is commending the pleasantries of trout-fishing to Chamberlain. Maynard studies Buckmaster's smooth face and smiles. Stanley and he have much in common he thinks. Both have humble ancestry within two past generations and Stanley too studied Math before pursuing his chosen profession of the law and entering public life. Both are in their own ways, social reformers but for the most part keep their mission covert. On occasion, they catch that look of mutual recognition in each other's eyes and nod to its tacit acknowledgement. They are on the same side.

The American Paul Cravath joins the table and begins to speak again to Maynard about the future interest rates of the agreed loans between their two countries. Maynard listens of course but his mind is mostly on their present progress. He strains to see the names of the stations and halts that they now speed through, counting down the miles before they reach the river. There is the village of Rue, the town of Larronville, of Flandre – seven miles to go, five, two… Then he sees the Somme in the near distance with its banks of green willow, gently meandering its way north-west to the sea across a flat, reclaimed land of marsh and drainage ditches.

The train slows as it approaches the simple timber trestle rail bridge. If it is intact and undamaged, they will cross without stopping.

The train keeps moving. Suddenly they are over.

As they regain speed and leave the river behind them, Maynard's eyes follow its route inland as it winds south towards the killing fields. Just a few miles away, its banks and surrounding fields are not green but of battlefield mud and dried blood, pitted with shell-holes and criss-crossed by makeshift footways of timber duckboards. Any surviving trees are blackened and skeletal. The members of the *Inter-allied Conference on Finance and Supplies* may be leaving these forsaken lands behind them but the opposing armies will remain here until one surrenders or is destroyed and yet more sons, brothers, husbands and fathers are released from their nightmare world. He looks away and redirects his mind to thoughts of Boulogne and home. There is not far to go. He returns to his conversation with Cravath and this time gives the discussion of multi-million dollar loans and shipments of gold bullion his full attention.

After a paltry lunch of Spanish omelette and bread, at around one-thirty, the outskirts of Boulogne can be seen in the distance. A half-hour later, the train pulls into the town's main station and decants the majority of its passengers out into the rain before moving on the short distance to the pier-side terminus and the end of the line. As the carriages empty and Maynard steps down onto the platform, he looks towards the front of the train and thinks he sees the back of the tall man he takes to be Alice's quarry and, not far behind him, the nurse herself. But they are but glimpses, most likely fretful imaginings. If indeed it was her, she is now gone, out of reach, lost in the crowd.

Whilst Chamberlain goes to the dockside telegraph office to inform Whitehall of their imminent departure across the Channel, Holmes and Maynard, aided by Booth and two Council secretaries, begin the process of transferring the bundles of art from the train's baggage car to the *SS Onward,* moored fifty yards away along the cobbled pier. It is a fraught business. The rain is now heavy and whilst the paintings will be kept dry, the Englishmen are quickly soaked and made cold. The dockside is crowded with ship's passengers and their luggage and the loading of goods and supplies. All seems in great disorganisation. What they can see of the rest of the harbour appears in a similar state of chaos, and everywhere porters, seamen and dockworkers scurry and look fretfully back towards the horizon for any sign of the approaching German army. Maynard had been hoping that the worst of their jeopardy was now behind them but is fast appreciating the wisdom of Alice's words. They would need their wits about them if they were to get safely back to England.

As they arrive at the foot of the *Onward's* gangway with the first of the art, the ship's broad-shouldered, sou-wester clad Bursar checks their papers and frowns as he surveys the rolls and crates of paintings.

"What's this lot then?" he asks.

"Paintings – art of great value. It belongs to the British Empire," says Holmes, showing the man the transit documents.

"I don't care overmuch 'oo it belongs to, it's not booked on and we've got no room for it. The 'olds are full."

The Bursar is a clean-shaven cockney in his mid-forties with the battered features of a bar-room brawler and a seen-it-all-before expression.

"There must be an extra storeroom on-board surely, for emergencies?" pleads Holmes.

"As you might be aware sir, the whole of the German army could come a-marching down that road at any time. This *is* an emergency."

Holmes is about to protest when Maynard puts his hand reassuringly on his friend's arm. He is saying 'let us rely on this man's good nature, we will leave him think on it for a while'.

Homes and Maynard stand in the drizzle, waiting for the verdict to come.

"'ow much of it is there anyway?" says the Bursar finally, after looking at the pile of art and considering the options.

"Another four medium-sized cases and eight more rolled bundles. Oh, and one rather large crate…"

"Stick it all under the lower deck canopy to start with, left at the top of the gangway," he says, giving in but not really listening to the detail of the inventory. He has the resigned eyes of someone who knows that these shenanigans will add to his burden of work today but that Maynard and Holmes seem like decent sorts who need a favour or two thrown in their direction. "Once we cast-off, you can move it all down to the aft day-cabin. Don't let the Captain be seeing you though, 'eel 'ave my guts for string bowties."

"Thank you, Bursar, thank you," says a relieved Holmes. "It really is …"

"Oh, and by the way gentlemen, we'll be leaving before the hour's out..."

Maynard pulls out his pocket watch, looks at Holmes and raises his eyebrows. That's in thirty minutes time.

"...we're part of a convoy and they won't wait. They've got hospital ships full of dying men," explains the Bursar.

The two friends understand. They nod their thanks then press on. After a frantic twenty minutes spent toing and froing between train and the boat, the transfer of the art is almost finished. Chamberlain has reappeared and as they are about to load the last of the bundles, he is waiting for them at the foot of the gangway

"Your labours are complete?"

"Not quite," says Holmes, "Norvin and Schwiter are still to come."

Chamberlain gives an understanding nod but looks like a man with bad news to tell.

"I've told Downing Street we should be in Folkestone by six o'clock. But they fear attacks on the railways tonight so they're sending motorcars to take us all up to London," he says before pausing. "And grim tidings from Paris. The Hun have revived their monster gun – two hundred people were killed there this morning."

Maynard and Holmes join Chamberlain in imagining the scenes of carnage but say nothing.

"I don't think we're quite in range here but we can't be sure. It's as well we're about to leave."

"We'll be aboard directly. Just the one last piece to put in place," says Holmes.

As Chamberlain turns and walks up the gangway, Holmes and Maynard return to the train for the final time. On the platform beside the baggage car, Booth and the secretaries have lifted the great case on to a commandeered handcart and Maynard and Holmes look on as the younger men carefully push the load out of the terminus building and across the cobbles towards the *SS Onward*. As they make their slow, cautious progress, Maynard becomes aware of the many dockside eyes now looking at them and their trundling seven-foot high wooden ark. He wonders again if German spies and saboteurs have tracked their progress from Paris and if Alice is safe. But the time for these concerns is past. He looks at his watch. There is just ten minutes left before embarkation.

They arrive at the foot of the narrow, slatted wooden gangway and then it hits them. By what method is the enormous crate to be got aboard? The Bursar stands on the quayside, hands on hips, a look of exasperated disbelief on his grizzled face. Maynard's heart sinks. How could this have been so ill-considered? The British army's *Seven Ps* adage jumps into his mind – that Proper Planning and Preparation Prevents Piss Poor Performance, but it is too late for self-recrimination.

Holmes spies a man in a black uniform dripping with the gold lace of officialdom just twenty yards away and makes one last desperate play. A short discussion confirms that the man is indeed a member of the Harbour Master's staff and even though Holmes explains the urgency of the situation, it is to little avail; the officer looks sympathetic but just shrugs. Holmes' plea that they are the *Mission Internationale* cuts no ice.

But the lessons learned in two days in Paris are not forgotten and Holmes reaches into his pocket to produce another fifty-franc note. As before, this oils the wheels of action and within a minute, the man has organised a small crane to be brought across the pier to the quayside next to the *Onward* and with its stabilising footings secured, their monster is lifted into the air and hoisted aboard.

Just as it touches-down on deck and the two Englishmen let out a shout of celebration, a low trolley, piled high with suitcases crashes through a stack of boxes on the other side of the pier and plunges into the water. All hell breaks loose as among the dockers and porters, insults fly and the idiot responsible is urgently sought. The *Onward*'s Bursar and two of his gangway crew rush across to be sure that there is neither injury nor loss of any of their ship's consignments. After five minutes, satisfied that all is well, they return to their duties as the last of the French loaders and officials leave the ship. Maynard, Holmes and the others walk wearily but smiling up the gangway and order drinks and sustenance in the ship's bar. As a final blast on the ship's horn signals its readiness to depart, Maynard looks one last time at the quayside, forlornly hoping to see Alice boarding, then slumps down in a wide armchair. His heart is racing and his movements are laboured. The words of his doctors return to him, their post-Diphtheria warnings of likely myocarditis and polyneuropathy – that his kidneys may sometimes falter. But this tightness in his chest has happened before. It is nothing, it will soon pass.

21

Across the Foaming Brine

When they cast off, Holmes does not join the others but instead goes to the day cabin where the art is to be stored. Some bundles are already there, carried through by members of the crew instructed to clear the decks. Alongside the paintings, in the corner of the cabin, lying supine on benches with basins and towels next to their improvised bunks, are General Mola and Guido, his secretary.

"Gentlemen, are you taken ill?" Holmes asks with genuine concern.

"The sea will be in turmoil, Mr Holmes, can you not feel it already?"

"No – is a storm expected? I heard it would only swell…"

"It will be the Devil's cauldron and as always on such seas, we shall be violently indisposed. But please Signore, do not worry," says the General as he rolls over, pulling a blanket across his face, "we will not vomit on your precious art. God forbid that any of it should be stained with our distress."

Holmes shrugs at this display of what he attributes to a foreigner's lack of moral fibre and sets about bringing through the rest of the paintings. On the deck, under Holmes' supervision, the Norvin-Schwiter monster crate is secured beneath a canopy by two deck hands and covered in a large blue tarpaulin. Now they are set.

Holmes goes to refresh himself, enjoying a bowl of vegetable soup and mullet in the ship's small restaurant, then adjourns to the salon. By the door, he finds a copy of yesterday's *Times* and seeing the back of Maynard's head in a nearby booth, joins his friend to see out the remainder of the crossing. As he walks across the caulked timber floor, the ship lists to port then violently tilts back to starboard, almost depositing him onto Maynard's lap. He steadies himself, stoops down to look out of window and sees that Boulogne is already just a dark line on the horizon. They have left the coastal shallows, gone around the hidden sandbars and must now be out in the deep Channel waters. The swell is without doubt increasing and a stiff rain-bearing south-westerly is catching the tops of five foot high waves, turning the sea to white spray.

Maynard sits with his eyes closed, his eyebrows knitted into a strained frown and whilst Holmes doubts his friend is asleep, he will not disturb his contemplation. Their absence of conversation is of no disappointment to him as there is much in *The Times* to digest – the latest War News, lists of awards of medals, the debate on whether the men in the ranks should be given their own drinking bars in the camps, the arrest of a War Department clerk in the US for the theft of ordnance plans...

Maynard is aware that someone has sat down and a glimpse through quickly opened-and-shut eyes confirms his friend's presence, but he does not wish to speak. Rolled by the pitch of the ocean, he is drifting into that half-state, somewhere between sleep and waking, and his mind is filling with scenes from the past days – the planning of the Degas coup at Charleston, his talk with Bonar Law, the frightened boulevards and empty streets of Paris and railway stations and trains full of the anxiety of war. But it is his remembrance of Alice which is most alive. Her eyes and sweet lips, the poignant scent of her makeup. He imagines a taut, white body beneath the straight lines of her duty uniform. It is a new promise which both excites and frightens him, like unlocking a door to a forbidden room. As the ship lurches again, he thinks that life's loves are not much dissimilar to being tossed by a volatile ocean and he resolves that if a future chance of safe, secure haven should arise, he will surely take it.

His eyes open a little and he spies Holmes immersed in the pages of his newspaper, smiling at something he is reading. Outside, the swollen, angry sea, rears and falls, its menacing rumble mingling with the throb of the ship's engines. He savours the last seconds of his tranquillity, that transitory nowhere where we are suspended in the void between dreams and the living world, then he speaks to his friend.

"Holmes?" he says, blinking himself awake. "Sorry, I have been asleep."

"My dear chap, are you alright? I was a little concerned but opted to let you rest."

"Yes, I'm quite well, thank you. I was down amongst the weeds of the subconscious," he says, stretching his arms.

"Ah, those unknowable depths beneath the water's surface!"

"And today I believe they are filled with English Channel cod fish," says Maynard, smiling at his friend just as the Bursar comes past, steadying himself on the high backrest of their banquette seating.

"Gentlemen, all of your paintworks safe and securely stowed I trust?" he says.

"We are in your debt sir. Your help was most essential to our enterprise. Please, sit with us a while."

The Bursar glances up at the salon clock and decides he can afford a few minutes of sociability.

"I shan't enquire as to the exact provenance of your art, sir, nor why it is being borne across the sea in the middle of a war. I'm sure you 'ave good and legal explanations," says the Bursar, touching the side of his nose.

"My friend had just speculated on what presently might be in the waters below us," replies Holmes, keen to change the subject.

"Apart from German mines and submarines?" the Bursar says as he sits down retaining his straight-backed demeanour.

Holmes and Maynard are not sure whether to laugh or frown and so remain expressionless.

"And then there are the wrecks of course," he continues. "*The Braunton,* sunk by a U-Boat in April of '16 just ten miles from here, the Cunard liner *Alaunia,* downed by a sub-laid mine. *The Mira* was an oil tanker, done-for last year by a mine left by UC-50 – the deadliest submersible to sail beneath these waters."

His audience of two say nothing, their smiles completely disappeared. But then the Bursar grins, having scared his compatriots to death, he now wishes to lighten the mood.

"The common fish you'll know about I'm sure but on the seabed, not just octopus, flounder and scallop but dab and fangtooth. And in the waters above them, spurdogs, thresher sharks and thornback rays."

Holmes and Maynard relax and find themselves drawn immediately into his image-making. Like the brothers in Millais' *Boyhood of Raleigh*, listening to the quayside stories of the fisherman, they are beguiled.

"Near the surface there'll be pilot whales and minkes too and when the season and currents are right, orcas. And I once saw a giant tuna, just two miles off the Cornish coast, near Lizard Point. She was chasing sardines I reckon. Sleek and silver-blue, seven feet long and cutting through the water at ten knots. A mighty hunter. Thank Christ they don't eat sailors! ...pardon my French," says the Bursar.

Holmes and Maynard sit in silence, savouring the light magic of the sailor's tales before Holmes brings them back to their current predicament, now, here, above the water line and in some jeopardy.

"And what news of the weather?" he asks.

"I fear we are already into a storm, sir," says the Bursar, standing up and looking out at the heaving water. "Not roaring bad but bad enough. But we hope for none of Jove's lightnings or dreadful thunder claps, *'nor fire and cracks of sulphurous roaring, the most mighty Neptune seem to besiege and make his bold waves tremble, his dread trident shake."*

Maynard and Holmes laugh and the Bursar acknowledges their light-hearted applause with a short bow.

"And I trust too that not *'all but mariners will quit the vessel and plunge in the foaming brine...*" adds Maynard, paraphrasing the remaining parts of the stanza.

But then the show is over. "I would recommend that in the event of catastrophe you stay well in the lifeboat, sir. If you were to fall in, even if you was to remain buoyant, the cold would soon 'ave you dead," says the Bursar, wagging a warning finger.

"Thank you. Most reassuring," says Holmes.

"Not at all sir," the Bursar replies, giving a sharp, ironic salute. "Oh, and it would be wise to stay here in the saloon. Keep your eyes fixed on the horizon – it is the best preventer of sea-sickness."

The next hour passes slowly in the absence of conversation and as the weather worsens, cutlery and crockery slide across tables and are eventually removed to safety. Some passengers crawl away to vomit, others skate across the floors before deciding that sitting still is the safest option. Maynard and Holmes remain silent until at last, as the afternoon light begins to fade, they see the Kent coast in the distance, glimpsed through the funnel smoke of the convoy ships ahead of them. They can be no more than two miles off-shore when there is the sound of a muffled explosion, near or far, it is hard to tell, followed by dull percussive thud below decks, the *Onward's* engines decelerate and there they are held, stationary, pitching and rolling in the great swell. The two men look at each other perplexed.

"Have the engines failed?" asks a twitching Holmes. Maynard doesn't answer but instead runs through the possible reasons for the stoppage and the probabilities of each resulting in terminal disaster. Ranking the list in order of likelihood – mechanical failure, wave damage, collision, sabotage, sea mine, canon, bomb, torpedo… Oddly, this makes him feel better.

"A submarine torpedo is the least likely cause of our predicament," he announces. If this analysis was intended to reassure Holmes, it doesn't work and his friend's jaw drops as he waits for the story behind this unwanted headline.

"For the past year, we have had new technologies – hydrophones, depth charges and special nets…" Maynard says, pausing as they are once again tossed sideways "…and our many surface search-craft have forced the Hun deeper into our anti-U-Boat mines…" He is forced to stop speaking again, this time bracing himself against the side of the booth as another strong wave hits the side of the ship. "As a result, I am told their submariners now take the northern route, around Scotland, before steaming into the Atlantic

236

to plunder our western approaches. It's the supply convoys they're really after…"

This serves only to cause Holmes' frown lines to deepen and he waves away Maynard's reassurances.

"We are like sitting ducks here," Holmes says, lowering his voice. "If not to submarines then to boat-launched torpedoes. Then there are the floating mines, German aircraft and the guns of battleships. If the Sea Devils were to cast their nets now, what a catch they would land. The world's Economists, Ministers of State, art's most precious wonders. First the train and now this."

"Steady old chap," says Maynard.

"To lose our hard-won purchases here, to the Hun and the sea, so close to home…"

Maynard now realises his friend's nerve fibres are beginning to shred.

"Come, let us see what is ahead of us," he says, standing up, holding tight to the handrail a-top the back of his seat. Holmes shakes his head, doubting the wisdom and the necessity of such a venture, but then grudgingly follows. They go up to the forward day cabin and peer out through the salt spray and rain to see two camouflaged hospital ships, Red Cross markings on their sides, heading into Folkestone harbour ahead of them.

Maynard nods. "They will need a good hour to disembark the wounded and for the dockside to clear. And we shall wait out here with patience and

237

gratitude, thankful that neither us nor our sons are amongst their number," he says.

"And I am most sorry," says a downcast Holmes. "I defeated sea-sickness but was instead laid low by fear. I believed I had vanquished him forever but he returned. You do not know him as well as I do I think."

"We have met once or twice and yes, he is an unwelcome visitor," says Maynard, putting a kind hand on his friend's stooped shoulder. "But we are nearly home."

Holmes lifts himself up and returns a grateful smile. Then the two men turn and lurch their way aft, past the pale-faced and the still retching.

22

Folkestone Harbour

At six o'clock, with the light fading fast and in cold teeming rain, the *SS Onward* gently bumps against the Folkestone Harbour Arm wall and secures its hawsers around black cast-iron bollards. The quayside is quite empty now, the hospital ships gone, unloaded and set off again to France to collect more distress and damaged goods.

On deck, the members of the Inter-ally Council gather with their bags and suitcases, awaiting Mr Berry's instructions to disembark and are greatly relieved not to be held long. Within five minutes, Chamberlain's promised fleet of London-bound Government cars can be seen snaking its way towards them along the pier. The convoy pulls up at the foot of the *Onward*'s gangway and the doors of the long-bodied Bentleys, Wolseleys and Rovers are opened as Berry calls out the names of the delegates who then scuttle forward, their coat collars turned up against the weather. The heavier luggage is portered-off and loaded into the cars' open boots.

Holmes and Maynard wait at the back of the queue, watching as their fellows pull away, waving stiff, gentlemanly farewells.

By six-thirty, Maynard, Holmes, Chamberlain and the inestimable Berry are the only members of the party who remain on board for it is they who will now oversee the loading of the paintings onto the waiting train, situated just thirty yards away on the pier. The precious bundles are transferred to the goods van quickly and without difficulty but the Norvin-Schwiter ark again proves impossible. The ship's deckhands who had disconnected it from the crane and manhandled it onto a trolley and across to the train, now stand perplexed, alongside a station guard, staring at the obviously too-narrow door. Holmes and Maynard hurry across and are greeted with the bad news.

"I've told the company about this wagon before, the opening's not broad enough. Your crate 'll have to wait for the next train sir," says the guard. "The nine o'clock service to Charing has a more manly goods van with wider doors. It'll fit through there for certain sure."

Holmes shakes his head, defeated, looking to Maynard for help.

"If needs must," says Maynard, giving his friend an encouraging nod. "Where can our crate be held until then?" he asks the guard.

"There's a canopy store, just a way down the pier, sir."

"It cannot be left there unattended," says Holmes, trying to keep his words private.

"I'll keep a good watch on it sir," says a voice from over Holmes' shoulder. It is their sole remaining trooper, his presence with them up until now quite unnoticed. "I'll oversee it onto the train then keep it company back to London."

"Thank you, sergeant, but should you now return to your unit?" says Maynard.

"Before he left for the Front, Captain Crimmond's last order was that I should stay with the Mission until all were safe home, including their cargos. That order still stands."

"Then we accept your help with great gratitude and are doubly in your debt," Holmes says, reaching out to shake the man's hand. The two make the respectful eye contact of brothers in arms.

"And you, Maynard, must journey back with Chamberlain and Berry, if they have no objection of course. You also have treasures to be kept safe," adds Holmes.

Chamberlain nods in agreement but Maynard hesitates, concerned that he will be abandoning both his friend and the booty.

"These works are now the property and responsibility of the National Gallery. Your job is done. We shall all meet again soon, back in London, after Easter," says Holmes reassuringly, as the luggage van door is slammed shut and the friends shake hands goodbye. All have now been assigned their final duties of care, to themselves and to the art.

"Better get aboard, sir," the guard warns Holmes as he unfurls his green flag and raises a whistle to his mouth.

As Holmes waves goodbye and the train pulls out of the quayside station, Chamberlain seeks out the Harbour Master's office from which to call Whitehall. Maynard stands watching until the last carriage is out of sight, silently wishing his friend and their hard-won gains an uneventful journey home. Ten minutes pass before an irritable-looking Austen Chamberlain returns, reporting that the phone lines are down for this entire part of Kent.

"Eastbourne is on the way to Charleston is it not?" he says, receiving a nod of confirmation from Mr Berry who, with Maynard beside him, is stood waiting beside the car. "We shall stop-off at the town's police station to telephone Whitehall that the mission is safely completed."

All three men clamber into Chamberlain's Bentley, their luggage and Maynard's paintings, now transferred to one of his suitcases, safely locked in the car's ample boot. As they are chauffeured away from the harbour and up through the town, Berry is quickly immersed in Government documents which he reads by torchlight whilst Chamberlain closes his eyes, his briefcase resting on his lap. Maynard stares out of the window. As they leave Folkestone by the high cliff road, in his peripheral vision he thinks he sees a flash of white light down in the harbour, at the end of the Arm Pier, where the *Onward* is moored. But looking back, he can make out nothing more and attributes it to tiredness. He starts to drift. He could sleep for a month.

242

23

A Sting in the Tail

Twenty minutes later, they pass through a small town which Maynard takes to be Hythe. It is difficult to tell as no house or pub lights can be seen in the darkness of the wartime blackout. Wherever it is, Charleston is still many miles away and Maynard rouses himself to bend Chamberlain's ear whilst he can. He leans towards his colleague and trying not to startle him, speaks softly but clearly.

"Austen...are you awake?"

"No."

"I'm sorry old chap but there's something I need to discuss."

"And what might that be?" replies a sleepy, disinterested Chamberlain.

"The future..."

"A big subject."

"...and what will become of the peace when the war is done."

Chamberlain now opens his eyes, blinks and looks at Maynard over the top of his glasses.

"Go on," he says.

"Having weighed up the various probabilities, I think it unlikely that France will be overrun or that the Germans will take control of the Channel coast."

"Well, that's a relief," says Chamberlain, jokily.

"If this were to happen they would surely shell London and we would be most right-royally rogered by a newly emboldened, priapic Hun."

"Agreed," says Chamberlain, trying hard not to show shock at Maynard's Bloomsbury tongue. Mr Berry quietly chuckles in the dark.

"If we can hold our ground against this current offensive, and with the United States to aid and abet us, I believe we will prevail – the war will be won perhaps six months hence, eight at most."

Chamberlain nods. He knows Maynard's predictions will be based on empirical data interrogated by relentless logic.

"But while there still exists the danger of defeat, there also sits a great threat concealed within our likely victory."

Both Berry and Chamberlain frown. Any expression of doubt on the likely success of the war effort smacks of defeatism and is not a prospect which can be discussed in Government circles, even in ironic jest. Maynard's private pacifism is well known but tolerated as long as he remains silent about it.

"Please, allow me to explain," he continues, sensing the alarm felt by his colleagues.

"If we win the war, no, *when* we win the war," he says, flashing a reassuring smile in Chamberlain's direction, "then there will be many voices clamouring for revenge, demanding punitive reparations for the damage inflicted by Germany, in particular those against the French nation."

"Which would be most understandable," says Chamberlain.

"Indeed – and we would all share the anger of those who have suffered so greatly. Hold those personally responsible to account but promote enlightened self-interest over widespread vengeance."

Maynard now has Chamberlain's undivided attention as he sets out the hypothesis which drives this plea.

"After the war, the world will be one of an interconnectedness not seen before in the history of civilisation – communications, transportation, ties of trade, investment and commerce will make it so. We shall, if you will, 'all be in it together'. To beggar your neighbour, to ruin him, however heinous his crimes and whatever the nature of the dispute, will be to beggar oneself and lead to pecuniary instability where only malevolence can grow."

"So you would have me speak out against reparations?"

245

"I have already spoken to others and many are similarly minded, Winston included."

"The British Government is to persuade victorious nations who have lost so much in lives and money to be magnanimous?"

"It would be in their own best interests and what is more, it would be most Godly."

"How so?"

"The policy of reducing Germany to servitude for a generation, degrading the lives of millions of human beings and depriving a whole country of happiness should be abhorrent and detestable to any Christian."

"I must agree," says Berry, unable to contain himself before swiftly backtracking. "Please, forgive my interruption."

Chamberlain accepts his Secretary's apology with a raised palm of understanding then gestures to Maynard to continue.

"And it would sow the decay of the whole of civilized life in Europe. We would risk pushing the German economy to breaking point, driving uncontrollable inflation, hyper-inflation even, and bring unemployment and political instability the likes of which Europe has not seen in a hundred years. There would be chaos – and such chaos hands the keys of the city to the devil."

Chamberlain sits in silence, allowing Maynard to finish his plea.

"Wars are not made by bad populations, only by bad politics. If we were to promote the policies of revenge, it would open the door to a new age of absolutism, to Hippias, Caligula and Genghis Khan, and ten, twenty years from now, who knows what weapons of death a dictator may have at their disposal. We have so far only glimpsed the horrors that mechanised war can bring."

Maynard is about to say more when Chamberlain finally raises his hand to block him.

"You ask much of us, Maynard, too much perhaps, but I know that you are right. I for one will do what I can in the cause of reconciliation, when the time is right."

Maynard smiles at his friend.

"That is all one ally can ever ask of another, to do what they can."

After this, the three men return to their own thoughts and drift as the car purrs through the Sussex night. Dymchurch, Rye, Hastings and Bexhill are passed and left behind, barely noticed. It is eight-thirty when they are jolted back into vocal consciousness by the ratcheting hand-brake being applied by their chauffeur and the engine switched-off.

"This is Eastbourne, sir. The Police Station is directly in front of us," he says. "Will you all be going inside?"

"Just me, driver, thank you,"

The confirmation causes the man to jump smartly out to open the passenger door as Chamberlain turns to Maynard. "This shouldn't take very long – I'm going to let Whitehall know that all's well with the Council members *and* the art. It's best if I speak to them as they may detect that you're keener on the welfare of the art than you are on the safety of the other members of the Council!"

Maynard smiles at Chamberlain as the door is closed and the three men settle down to await his return. Ten minutes pass as Berry naps and Maynard gazes out through the car window at what he can see of the deserted Eastbourne streets. The occasional vehicle headlight illuminates a nearby billboard poster for the Devonshire Park Winter Gardens and Pavilion. Tomorrow will be Good Friday. He'd lost track of the days. Life goes on. Next week, Devonshire Park orchestra will accompany the popular baritone Jackson Potter and the celebrated *Ronez Quartette*. From 11.00 a.m. until 1.00 p.m. there will be roller skating, with music. In the Pavilion they will show the new Charlie Chaplin film, *The Floorwalker*. How amusing the little man is. Maynard wonders if they'll get the chance to see the film in London or in Lewes over the coming week. The advertisement tells him also that *The Gay Lord Quex* is to be presented soon. He knows that the original 1899 play on which the cinema film was based sparked much controversy and was regarded by many as an immoral tale. How things change! – no-one now would so much as raise an eyebrow of disapproval in this current permissive, modern age. It is the humorous story of a philanderer who tries, through many trials and tribulations, to become monogamous. In the end, Quex is reformed. True love it seems can amend our very natures.

Maynard is beginning to drift off to sleep again when the car door opens and Chamberlain re-joins them.

"Thank you, driver, we can continue onto Charleston House now…near Firle, I believe?" he says, looking to Maynard for confirmation. Maynard nods. "Yes, Firle. Off the Lewes road."

Chamberlain slides the dividing window between driver and passengers tight shut then sits in silence after the car pulls away.

"I seem to forever be the bearer of bad news," he sighs after a full minute.

"What is it now pray?" asks Maynard.

"Tales of grave misfortune but some good luck too in evidence, mostly ours."

Maynard doesn't like the sound of this and is bracing himself for the worst as Chamberlain begins his report.

"Whitehall is pleased and relieved that we are almost safe home – they had feared catastrophe had befallen us."

Berry and Maynard hang on his every word as the Bentley leaves the outskirts of town behind and speeds west along the open coast road.

"There was a submarine attack earlier today, out in the Channel, not far from our position. A cargo ship called the *TR Thompson* was torpedoed and 33 of its crew were killed. The reports say the vessel was struck on the nose and that she opened up like a tin can and sank within minutes."

Maynard and Berry say nothing, waiting for the rest of it.

"And the *SS Onward* too is stricken. It must have happened just after we left her. A fire caused by a thermite bomb concealed in the life jackets by enemy agents they think. The crew had to open the sea valves to scuttle the ship onto her side to prevent the blaze from spreading to the pier. The Bursar, our brave trooper sergeant and others are feared lost, putting out the flames, trying to save lives. We must assume that the Norvin and Schwiter paintings are also gone."

"How could the Germans have got aboard?" asks Berry.

"A diversion," says Maynard. "That incident on the quayside distracted the Bursar and his crew. The saboteurs' getting on and off the boat was easy, adjusting the timers on the fuses thankfully proved more difficult for them."

"The army are linking it to a nest of vipers discovered in Boulogne's harbour town, just before we set sail. A group of their saboteurs were cornered by French troops led by one of our SIS people. But a villain or two must have escaped and got through to the pier."

Maynard freezes.

"The British agent was a woman, killed they say, but the reports are confused. You know how cagey that fellow Cumming is about releasing too much in the way of detail."

They complete the rest of the journey in dark silence. Maynard will of course seek confirmation, send urgent telegrams as soon as his attendance at the Treasury allows it. He believes in no God but still prays that the reports prove unreliable, exaggerated, mistaken – that Alice is safe, the truth obscured by the fog of war.

24

Return to Charleston

Thirty minutes pass before Maynard slides open the glass hatch and gives the driver an instruction to pull off the main road. The car moves cautiously up a cartwheel-rutted lane under overhanging trees before arriving at the open gate to Charleston Farmhouse. As the Bentley starts to turn in, its headlamps reveal a rough, wet track and they come to a jarring halt.

"Begging your pardon, sir, but the car 'll not go any further, not through all that mud it won't," says the chauffeur to Maynard. "Our weight would sink us before we got ten feet. We'd need a Mark Five tank, ditching beam 'n all, to pull us out again."

"That's quite alright driver, I can walk from here."

"If you're sure, your Lordship..."

The man is forgiven and reassured and Maynard turns to Berry and Chamberlain with a broad smile of goodbye. He will now do his best to put to one side his concerns for Alice. He must be a brave soldier, as she would want him to be.

"Gentlemen, it has, as always, been a pleasure to share your company and I am most grateful for your assistance in our Degas coup. We shall reconvene in Whitehall next week."

No hands are shaken – they work together and office etiquette forbids it.

"Can we not at least help take your luggage to the door?" asks Berry, as the driver opens Maynard's passenger door.

"No, thank you. There will be a hundred yards of sodden earth and muck to brave and you must be on your way to London without reeking of dung."

Maynard closes the door shut as the chauffeur unloads his luggage, delivers a short salute and wishes him goodnight. Then, as the Bentley swings around to return to the main road, Maynard looks down at the pile of bags and realises the scale of the challenge ahead. Judging by the state of the track, it must have been raining here for days. At least it has now ceased and there is just enough moonlight to see the way ahead but carrying all the burdens at the same time is quite out of the question. He will take what he can and return for the rest. As his briefcase and holdall contains much Government work, they will take the priority and he will seek help in bringing home the paintings.

He finds a discrete hole under a hedgerow, close to the gate post, then secretes the suitcase of art before standing back to survey the scene to ensure it is not obvious to passers-by. Not that there are likely to be many such persons on the lane at this hour, it being several miles from Lewes town on an unpleasantly damp March night. But to lose the great works now through carelessness...

The walk to the house is most trying and he stops frequently to catch his breath. Every third step one foot or the other plunges into a water-filled rut or else it is sucked into the sticky mud. The whole experience puts him in mind of life at the Treasury. There is much lurching from side-to-side in cloying conditions, equilibrium is often disturbed and every step forward, no matter how small, requires a Herculean effort. Then, just when it seems that good progress is being made, one is wrong-footed by an unseen hazard which threatens to upend you. On the dry road of *máthēma* though, his feet skip over the firm ground in a gravity-defying, high-stepping dance. He can leap, pirouette, even cartwheel as the mood or interest takes him. Perhaps that is his real future. One should go where the going is easy.

Now he looks up. The house is still fifty yards away. Onward, onward.

He squelches forward and thinks again of his just ended conversation with Chamberlain. He is a sorry to have delivered his sermon in such confined claustrophobia after the day they have all had, but needs must. If the victorious Allies pursue an attritional route to compensation from Germany, he will resist, protest, resign from Government and write of the damnable economic and political consequences of such a peace. But will anyone listen? They must. The ideas of the economist and the political philosopher are more powerful than is commonly understood, indeed the world is ruled by little else. Even self-seeking commercial interest will eventually be beaten back into its corner by the potency of *ideas*, by a unifying vision of how better the world might be. Practical men who believe themselves to be exempt from any intellectual influence are unknowingly the servants of some half-forgotten classical philosopher or economist. Madmen in authority who hear voices in the air, are unknowingly distilling their frenzy from some academic scribbler of the past. Such people may not understand the history of such things but he, John Maynard Keynes, does. He knows that the intellectual construct will always, in time, triumph over low animal spirit.

Then, suddenly, he is home. Beside Charleston's low garden gate, he stands for a few reflective seconds then exhales a long breath of satisfaction. In the sky above, menacing clouds roll in over the black mass of Firle Beacon but the house windows glow with warmth. He is safe. It is done. Exhausted, he struggles to open the gate and staggers a little as he walks forward. He is just five steps from the front door when it suddenly opens and the hallway light floods out to greet him. Duncan emerges warily, straining to see who is there.

"I'm sorry to startle you, I couldn't telegram to say when I'd be returning," says Maynard, dropping his bags before almost falling into Duncan's arms.

"My darling man, you are returned!" he exclaims, supporting his friend and hugging him in great relief. "We have heard the reports of Paris under siege and a German offensive covering half of France. I would be lying if I said we had not feared for you."

"There was no need, it will take more than siege guns and storm troopers to kill *me* off!"

Duncan smiles as he releases his friend but then puts his hand on Maynard's shoulder and looks hard into his sleep-deprived eyes. "Was it very terrible, there in France?"

"For many, yes."

"And were you in grave danger?"

"Not really, but our brave soldiers died in their thousands in the ferocity," he says, dwelling in momentary respect for their loss before pushing such thoughts again to one side. For a second he worries he is becoming anaesthetised, war-weary and immune to the horror, that he is himself now suffering a fatigue of mourning.

"...and then there was the trauma of Inter-Ally Council," he says, lightening the conversation. "It had much in common with a badly played game of Bridge and its outcomes were of similar small consequence. There were many things left undone and I will have to work some hours on the next steps, starting tomorrow. Sorry."

"Of course, but that is for the morning. For now, come in and drop anchor in your favourite armchair," says Duncan, helping to carry Maynard's luggage into the hall before nervously popping the question he has been waiting to ask. "And how went the auction?"

"We were moderately successful," Maynard says, with smug understatement as he takes off his coat.

"You bought all the paintings we asked for?!"

"Not all, some."

"Some?"

"Upwards of twenty I think. Holmes is taking them now to Trafalgar Square by train."

"Twenty! Then you are our hero and beauty's champion too."

"And I shall accept the honour but before that, if someone would like to go down to the end of the track, there's a Cezanne just behind the gate."

Duncan is open-mouthed in disbelief.

"And others too, in my brown suitcase. An Ingres, Monsieur Delacroix's *Cheval au Paturage* and a small *Study*. That is for you, if you'd like it that is."

"Dearest friend..."

Duncan hugs him again but as he does so, knows that there is more, much more to this adventure than Maynard will ever tell him or anyone else. He

257

is bound by his oath of Official Secrets but it is also the nature of the man himself. Though he uses a great many words, he wishes to be judged more by his actions. He will keep his recollections to himself. *Facta non Verba*.

"I shall fetch my coat and then Monsieur Cezanne!" says Duncan, putting down the last of the bags and shouting the news of Maynard's arrival to the others. "Nessa saw the car headlights from upstairs and called out that we might have visitors. She will be most relieved to see you – there have been sleepless nights. If you had been lost, she would have thought it her fault for cajoling you into going to the auction and into such danger."

"She cannot take all the credit, first and foremost, I blame you!" Maynard says with a smile as Duncan grabs his jacket from its boot room hook. "And let's not forget Roger, the original plotter. And half the Treasury thought it a most meritorious idea. I was just a naïveté executing the ideas of others, a marionette in the hands of master puppeteers."

Duncan laughs and gives Maynard a playful pat on the back before dashing away to retrieve a king's ransom's worth of Fine Art, stuffed under a Sussex hedgerow.

Maynard drags his weary self into the small sitting room next to the hallway and sinks down into an armchair. He isn't sure which he feels in most urgent need of – sleep or sustenance. He settles for a cigarette and draws in the smoke in a long, slow inhalation. In the soft-lit room, his eyes quickly start to close before he hears the sound of Nessa's short, urgent steps.

"And where pray is our brave Perseus, our Jason, and is he returned with a Golden Fleece or two?" she is saying as she comes bustling through the doorway. Maynard rises and feels the warmth of her sisterly embrace around him. After three breaths' worth of time, he starts to release his arms but she holds on to him tightly. Another five pass by before she steps away, wiping small tears from her eyes.

"There was no need to fret," he says gently. "Neither our art nor my life were ever in danger."

"So now, tell me everything," she says, pulling her sensible self together as the sound of the returning Duncan is heard in the hallway. "Firstly, whose motor did I see at the gate, the one which brought you home to us?"

"Austen Chamberlain's. It was good of him to take such a detour, damn good. I'm afraid I repaid him by delivering a lecture on the dangers of the peace, when it comes. I shall apologise when I see him next week in Whitehall. There will be no holidays for me at present."

"And the auction?" she says excitedly.

They sit down and Maynard begins his tale as Duncan joins them. He has unpacked Maynard's suitcase and now places the brown paper-wrapped package of paintings on the small writing desk in the corner of the room. Bunny and Clive appear, greet Maynard with warm handshakes and gather round. They all look quizzically at the bundle but ask no questions, allowing Maynard to commence the story. He fills in more of the detail than already given to Duncan, telling them of Petit's saleroom and their initial

259

reconnaissance, Holmes' auction craft, the expenditure and of what they have bagged for the National Gallery – the Gauguin, Manet's Wife and her Cat, the Corots and the Ingres, the huge Norvin and Baron Schwiter and all the rest. He says nothing of his concern for the fate of the big crate nor of the peril of the past days – of the bombing of trains, the threats from submarines and mines or of the shelling from monster guns.

"It was most excellently done, the National Gallery will surely name an entire wing after you!" says Clive.

"Our world is yours as is everything in it. And what is more, you are our man again, my son," adds Bunny, smiling cheekily as he puts a congratulatory arm around Maynard.

Nessa is pleased but not delighted. Some of Holmes' reported efforts have disappointed her and she frowns.

"It was well executed, of course, but he wasted many chances I believe," she says. "He missed an El Greco, refused a Cezanne and returned home with £5,000 still unspent."

"Conditions were not ideal my love – their hands were tied by circumstance and the presence of Chamberlain in whose gift the signed cheques were..." remonstrates Duncan.

"And now, shall we open our presents?" Maynard interjects cheerily. It is a pre-emptive strike of distraction, ensuring that nothing boils over between Nessa and Duncan. It has been a long day.

"And what have you bought us?" asks Nessa as Maynard goes across to the parcel and begins to undo the string and wires, using the desk letter-opener to cut-through the tough brown paper wrapping.

"Great works for our private pleasure," he says with a flourish.

"Tell me their names," she demands, standing up excitedly. "Quickly, before I leap on them and tear off all their clothes!"

"Patience dear girl, you will see everything soon enough," he says as he slowly, carefully, removes their final garments, revealing each picture to admiring purrs of pleasure and admiration. Holmes' parcellings were done most expertly and all are in fine, undamaged condition.

It is the Cezanne which is kept until last and as it is unveiled, the friends crowd forward, each moving, tilting, scrutinising the changing effects of the light on the exquisite brushwork. Nessa allows a single word to escape under her breath, speaking more to herself than to the others.

"Amazing," she says.

The little oil, just seven inches by ten, shows green and red apples on a neutral, brown table cloth, and is rich both in beauty and in meanings most profound. To Christians, apples are a symbol of the earth and the cosmos and are markers of meaningful human events, the cycle of existence and the fruit of exchange between Adam and Eve. Here, tonight, the image betokens the sharing of the love between them and speaks of an affinity to the simple life, a love of the rolling chalk Downlands and the countryfolk of the Sussex Weald just as Cezanne had an affection for the Provencal workers of the land, something that he never felt for the fashionable well-to-do of Paris.

"The National Gallery may have missed buying Monsieur Cezanne, but I did not. My new career has begun – I am become a collector!" Maynard says, with a wide smile. Then, like happy children, the five friends dance in celebration with conjoined hands and laughter.

25

Home at Last

On the train up to London, Charles Holmes sits alone in the First Class dining car and has a weird supper of tongue and coffee. All the carriages are near-empty so late on this Good Friday eve as those who would be away for the Easter weekend are already arrived at their destinations and few will move again now until after the holiday. Deserted stations flash past like photographs, scenes frozen in time, as the train speeds north-westwards. Staring out into the night, Holmes ponders what the future holds for him on his return to Trafalgar Square.

Whatever others may think, the Directorship of the National Gallery is no comfortable sinecure – the post-holder is most regularly a target of envy and the victim of political crossfire. Parliamentary enemies and social rivals of the Gallery's Trustees mischievously and always erroneously, put about rumours that Holmes thinks them uneducated and interfering. Fellow-painters resent any accolades he may receive as an artist of merit, putting such praise down to him now being a member of an inner establishment circle of critics and wealthy patrons. They claim too that he is not cognizant of the concerns of the broader arts community, that he cares little for the opinions of his peers or for their views on the future of British painting.

He has to admit that regarding his natural reluctance to engage in wider discussion, they have a point. But in his defence, he must say that whilst he can be impatient and wish to do things his own way, there are often insufficient hours in the day to do more than attend to his immediate duties. There is no time for consultation. There a great many official documents and memoranda to be read, circulated and answered, many from Downing Street and the Cabinet itself. The National Gallery is, after all, owned, run by and accountable to, the Government of the day. Routine matters have to be dealt with promptly, efficiently and, during the troubled days of war, urgently. The storage of precious art away from the London bombings, budgetary and staff losses, ongoing questions about the attribution and suitability of pictures planned for public display, the investigation of possible future acquisitions... the list goes on. Sometimes just the thought of it induces the cruellest of migraines and he has increasingly sought remedy in the peacefulness of his Lake District home at Appleby.

He wonders if, after the war is over, some of the criticisms levelled at his imagined autocracy will be headed off by placing him under a Chairman, a new post which will relegate the Director to a more subordinate role. Though publicly belittling perhaps, such a development might be a blessing in disguise. His power to curate is already much diminished compared to his predecessors and his latest ambition, using the experience he gained in the publishing business to produce catalogues on the Gallery's holdings as well as a new guide book, would only be helped by such a move. Some clouds can have silver linings.

As they approach Sevenoaks, with the future now looking much more to his liking and his food and drinks finished, Holmes happily drifts off to sleep and it is only when the train jolts to a halt at signals on the outskirts of London that he is again awake. They will be at Charing in less than a half-hour.

At New Cross Gate, he goes to the back of the train so as to be at the nearest door to the baggage car when his charges are unloaded. As they get closer to the metropolis' centre, rumbling along the high-level line into London Bridge, he sees that the city below him lies in utter darkness with barely a single vehicle headlight to be seen in the streets. Beyond the Thames' wharf buildings, the river itself is empty of lighted traffic and is but a wide band of black nothingness. Peril is still **ever-present** in the closing hours of their adventure, all London fearing bombs from the air or, he imagines, the possibility of the super-gun's long-range shelling if the Germans have now overrun the French coast, its fire directed by stealthy, Zeppelin-borne observers. But then he steadies himself, his concern now is to get the paintings safely to the National then wait for the Manet and the Delacroix to arrive. He must still keep his nerve.

As the train passes Waterloo then crosses the river into Charing Cross, he thinks of their great crate still on Folkestone pier and looks at his watch. It is just before nine o'clock. If all has gone according to plan, they would have loaded it onto the train by now and it would be ready to start its journey to London. He crosses his fingers for its safe transit.

The platforms at Charing are quiet but he still manages to find enough porters who, with the promise of generous tips, help him transport the bundles of art and his own suitcases, by trolley and by hand, the three-hundred yards down The Strand and around Trafalgar Square to the Gallery's lower eastside door. Holmes rings the night porter's bell and waits under a dim light for someone to attend the call. Eventually a postcard-sized hatch in the door is slid back to reveal a man's face, his hard, sharp eyes glowering out to see who it is that bothers him at this hour.

"Good evening Mr New. Whatever are you doing on duty at this time of night?" asks Holmes.

"Mr Holmes is it? I could very well ask you the same, sir," the man replies, pushing the hatch shut before opening the heavy door.

"We have new acquisitions to deposit," announces Holmes, pointing at the wrapped paintings before gesturing to the station porters to follow him inside. "Is there room here in the cellar for these, just until we can find somewhere better?"

"I should think so but where's it all come from and what..."

"It's a long story, Mr New," says Holmes, as he walks along the stone-floored corridor to four barrel-roofed brick side vaults. Each is some eight feet wide and of the same height, and all are lined with racks and shelving. Pointing the depositories out to the station porters, Holmes then supervises the storage of the packages and bundles, gives each man his promised ten shillings and his thanks, then follows them back to the entrance.

"My personal luggage I shall also leave here and will return again in two hours with one last delivery. It is a crate, a rather large one I'm afraid," Holmes says, surveying the cellar space. "We can stand it at the far end there, next to the wall."

"Very good, sir. As I've no other plans this evening, I shall wait up for you."

"Good man," says Holmes with a smile, "and now I shall adjourn to the Reform Club to rest for a short time. Let us hope I do not fall asleep and miss my train."

"Beg your pardon, sir?"

"I'm sorry, a poor joke with myself."

"I can see that you're tired, Mr Holmes. May I suggest that you share your intended arrangements with the doorman at your club so that he can ensure the satisfactory expedition of your plans?"

"Thank you – that is much appreciated good advice and I shall follow it."

The door is closed behind Holmes and he makes his way down to Pall Mall and up the steps of the Reform Club. It too is in semi-darkness with only a handful of late-staying members still in its dining rooms and bars. He explains to the porter the nature of his mission and that he must leave again by ten-thirty at the latest. If necessary, he must be awoken and pointed back in the direction of Charing Cross station. Then, longing to rest, he walks slowly into the Italianate Saloon, finds himself a quiet corner and lies down. But he dare not sleep and tries to keep himself awake by recalling some of the amusing past histories of this place – Verne's Phileas Fogg both beginning and ending his fictitious adventure to circle the globe in eighty days, here at the Reform. How this very room was the scene of his friend Robbie Ross's feud with Lord Alfred Douglas, that Bram Stoker and Henry Irving, royalty of the theatre, mingled here with the liberal bankers Rothschild and Goldschmidt. Thackeray, Henry James, H.G. Wells and Arnold Bennett treated the place as a second home. Just last year, Holmes himself was here at lunch when on the next table the poets Owen and Sassoon met and were joined by Roddy Meiklejohn, Maynard's principal Whitehall supporter in their mad escapade to the Degas auction. What was it they spoke of – did Sassoon show the others rough drafts of some future poem about the horror of war? As exhaustion overwhelms him and he slips into unconsciousness, broken stanzas fill his mind, scrambled by unreliable memory.

Have you forgotten yet?
The coming dawn, dirty-white, chill with a hopeless rain...
...the doomed and haggard faces...the fading, dying eyes,
The masks of the lads who once were so keen and kind,

Do you ask, "Is it all going to happen again?"

"Mr Holmes, I'm sorry," says a voice in his head. For a few moments he thinks he is still in his dream.

"Please... sir, it is almost eleven o'clock."

Holmes blinks and wakes up.

"Nearly eleven you say? Strewth man, can you not follow a simple instruction. The shipment will have arrived and may now be abandoned," he shouts, leaping up from the chaise longue.

"You were slid right down sir, out of sight. We searched but you were nowhere to be found..."

The porter's words fade behind him as he dashes back towards the entrance hall as fast as a plump, desk-bound fifty-year-old could manage. Within three muscle-straining, gasping minutes, he has covered the seven hundred yards between the Reform Club and Charing Cross and arrives on the concourse to seek out the train which according to the station clock must now have arrived from Folkestone. But no, it is not at the same platform on which he came in and there is no notice on the information board which at this time of night, appears unmanned. After five minutes of panic, he finds a porter who tells him of fires and incidents at Folkestone Harbour pier station, delays to the train, but of its imminent arrival at platform 1. He rushes to find it already there, its passengers apparently long since disembarked. At the far end of the train, he sees their Degas ark sitting on the platform, their weary-looking trooper guardian sitting slumped beside it on a platform bench.

"My dear chap, I am most sorry to be late..." says a breathless Holmes, as soon as he is within speaking distance of the soldier. The man's appearance shocks him into an unintended exclamation.

"Holy Christ, what has befallen you?"

The soldier's uniform is soot-blackened, stained and in places, torn. His face and hands have cuts and scratch marks and despite his best efforts to clean himself up, his skin is filthy.

"A fire, on the *Onward*, part was extinguished but they scuttled her to save the pier. She turned over and went part-under, right there in the harbour."

Holmes darts an involuntary, anxious look at the crate.

"The paintings were most fortunately far enough away and the flames did not reach them or the pier station. There was great chaos though."

"And by the looks of it, you were in its midst."

"I am well sir, just in need of a bath and a good sleep."

"Then please, take this," says Holmes, handing the trooper a five-pound note. "Use it to taxi yourself back to barracks, or to your home, or to pay for a night here in town. You are a hero and I shall ensure that Mr Keynes shall report the same to your commanding officer."

The two shake hands and as the soldier walks away, Holmes begins once more to scan the platforms for urgent assistance but there is now little activity as the station winds down for the night and the Easter weekend. Nervously leaving the great crate unattended, he takes a full ten minutes to first locate the Station Master's office before spending more precious time persuading a young but most un-willing Deputy to assist him. Again, Holmes' International Mission credentials prove useful leverage although, once more, it is the offer of additional reward which secures a large handcart, two lanterns and four press-ganged porters.

With the precious cargo safely secured on its flat framed wooden bier, they move off in the manner of a solemn cortege, out across the dark forecourt and over the cobbles, past the Eleanor Cross to a Trafalgar Square lit now only by the waning moon and the glow of their carriage lamps.

At the National, Mr New dutifully opens up the side door again and their burden is most carefully steered inside, unbound from its cradle and lifted into a position of safe repose against the wall of the cellar vault. Holmes thanks, remunerates and bids goodnight to the porters before Mr New is informed that he will see him again in the a.m. of the Tuesday of next week. Happy Easters are exchanged before the heavy iron door is shut and bolted closed and Holmes turns and walks away, satisfied, to return himself to his wife and children. Back at Charing, he finds a taxi to take him north to Hampstead and after climbing inside, notices the vehicle maker's mark and smiles to himself. It is a *Panhard & Levassor*, another French import.

271

Sixty miles away to the south, at Charleston House, John Maynard Keynes lies in bed alone under white linen sheets, restless in the dark. He hopes the last of the paintings, still locked inside their great wooden cocoon, have safely arrived into Holmes' care and now repose in some quiet corner of the National Gallery. Perhaps though, they are nothing but smoking ashes or lie under thirty feet of sea water in Folkestone Harbour. He will telegram his friend tomorrow and receive reports of woe and damnable bad luck or else glad tidings of relief.

Maynard curses himself that on the last leg of the race, too much was left to chance, that he should and could have done more. But then remembering that self-reproach is the price we all must pay for having control of our own destinies, he smiles. He recalls too that the adoption of such practical precepts is very distant from the optimism of a cosseted youth spent in a paradise, an edenic heaven where all was predetermined and, for good or ill, was surely for the best. For a moment, he mourns that lost innocence. The war's tumult has proven to them all that God does not always choose benevolence and that Eden requires much care and cultivation even if, in the end, we are undone by capricious fate. His mind drifts into soft thoughts of Alice, who at another moment of the world might have loved him. Then, falling into sleep, as if turning the pages of some childhood picture book, he sees himself borne forward through the years towards a light in some high window, far away.

Author's Note

"A Spark of Mild Adventure" was how Sir Charles Holmes, the Director of the National Gallery between 1909 and 1916, described the perilous journey he and Keynes made to Paris in late March 1918. Their adventure was, of course, anything but 'mild' and it is this modest section of his 1936 auto-biography, *Self & Partners*, which forms the thread of this dramatic story, here told for the first time in novel form; part historical account, part wartime thriller — a work of fiction woven from fact.

Most of the events recounted in this book actually happened and the main characters were real people. Some alterations to the chronology, and the invention of one or two of the supporting cast, have been carried out for storytelling purposes. The dialogue is of course largely invented but in places, parts of letters, telegrams and diaries are used but intended to sit seamlessly within the text. The art history descriptions and commentaries are, I hope, correct. We have tried to spot and fix any typos, spelling mistakes and bad grammar, incorrect or overlooked source references etc. but inevitably, one or two may have slipped through the net. Apologies for those.

In order to recreate the atmosphere of the period, an Edwardian style of prose and dialogue has been adopted. This has meant using an omniscient narrator and writing in a way which, to our present sensibilities, might in places appear overly wordy and oddly formal, often *telling* as well as *showing*. To enhance the effect further, the adventure novels of authors including Rider Haggard and Erskine Childers have been an influence.

In 1918, Modernist *stream of consciousness*, 'authentic' literature was still in a fledgling state and although James Joyce and Dorothy Richardson had been published, the perspective and attitudes of the characters portrayed in this story remain rooted firmly in the nineteenth century.

When I was at school, my mother decided I should get the best possible grades in Mathematics and so arranged for me to have extra coaching from a retired public school master friend of hers, Ernest Lionel Raymond. At the time of my first exams in 1968, he was in his eighties and had been a contemporary of Keynes at Cambridge, like him studying Math. As he came from a similar social background to Keynes, my recollections of Ernest's world view, manner, vocabulary and speech patterns (always delivered in mellifluous *Goodbye Mr Chips* tones), were extremely helpful in the writing of this book. This personal connection to a past world is one of many things he bequeathed to me and I should like to dedicate this story to him with gratitude for his kindness, patience and diligence. Like John Maynard Keynes, he believed it was his bounden duty to leave the world a better place than he found it.

DES, Oxfordshire 2022

John Maynard Keynes

1883 – 1946

In his 1905 philosophical treatise *A Theory of Beauty*, the twenty-two year old Keynes analysed the power of great art to delight the senses, nourish the soul and renew the human spirit. He concluded that the contemplation of artistic beauty would always "give rise to a state of mind which is good". Becoming a member of the Contemporary Arts Society in 1911, the man who would later become the first chair of the Arts Council of Great Britain, thought it was the duty of the state to provide access to art for every citizen, rich and poor, and that as part of the education process this would lead to enlightenment, social progress, and greater shared prosperity and happiness.

After graduating with a First Class degree in Mathematics from Cambridge, Keynes also schooled himself in Applied Economics and Probability Theory. He quickly showed an aptitude for solving practical problems through the application of advanced math and economics and had careers as both a Civil Servant and as an academic. He was also a scholar of Classical cultures, philosophy and Fine Art, making frequent visits to the Louvre in Paris in the years before World War 1. He and his Bloomsbury Group friends who included Virginia Woolf, her sister Vanessa Bell and husband Clive, E.M. Forster, Dora Carrington and Lytton Strachey, devoted themselves, as Keynes put it, to "the creation and enjoyment of aesthetic experience," and believed that the sophistication of any nation could be measured by the beauty of the art it produced and owned. France, and Paris in particular, was widely regarded as having the finest collections of art in the world and would have been looked upon with envy by many English artists and curators.

Just days before the outbreak of war in 1914, the British Government had urgently hired Keynes to serve as a young Treasury economist, helping the government to fund the war effort whilst also lending heavily to France and other allies to keep them from financial collapse. Still only 31, he devoted himself to this cause for the next four years, working (as he later wrote) "with the immense anxieties and impossible financial requirements of those days." He was made a Companion of the Order of the Bath, a form of Knighthood, by King George V in 1917 for his war work at The Treasury.

As the Head of External Finance at the British Treasury and a member of the International Finance Mission, Keynes had to travel to Paris in the spring of 1918 to attend crucial talks on the allied funding of the war. But he other purposes which were both patriotic and personal. Through art critic Roger Fry and his friend Duncan Grant, he had learned that a treasure trove of the world's finest paintings, originally owned by Edgar Degas, was to be auctioned at the Galerie Georges Petit and hoped that some of the collection might be obtained at bargain prices for Britain's National Gallery. He believed that by bringing home a collection of French 19th Century and Impressionist art, at that time unrepresented in the national collection, he would be investing in his country's cultural future as well as winning his way back into the good graces of his pacifist, vehemently anti-war friends in the Bloomsbury Group. On March 26th and 27th 1918, paintings by Manet, Gauguin, Cezanne, Corot, Ingres, Delacroix and others were auctioned in the sale on the Rue de Seze. Having survived several near-misses on the journey to Paris as the train skirted the battlefields of the Somme, and facing the prospect of an equally dangerous return channel crossing avoiding enemy mines and warships, in the salerooms with the sound of exploding German shells in the background, Keynes still had the presence of mind to use his own money to bag a few masterpieces for himself. By the end of his life, he had bought 135 paintings at a cost of £12,800; art that today would be valued at £76 million. One of the most influential British figures of the twentieth century and a champion of noble causes, he was also ever the shrewd investor.

Following the Armistice, he was present at the Versailles Peace Conference of 1919, counselling in vain not to set punitive war reparations on Germany as he feared that this would lead to economic collapse, destabilisation and further armed conflict. It gave him no satisfaction when, twenty years later, he was proved right.

Most academics agree that Keynes' thinking still influences the fiscal policies of governments the world over. It was Keynesian Economics which provided President Barack Obama with the theoretical framework he needed to justify spending three-quarters of a billion dollars stimulating the US economy in order to deal with the financial crisis of 2007-2008. The vital role played by the state in helping many businesses to survive the Covid-19 pandemic, is also Keynesian in origin.

He was instrumental in the founding of what were to become some of the great institutions of modern life – the National Health Service, the World

Bank and the IMF, the Arts Council and the National Theatre and was a lifelong supporter and benefactor of the Royal Opera House, Sadler's Wells ballet, the Cambridge Arts Theatre and many other community arts and public literacy projects. Shortly after the events described in this story occurred, he met and fell in love with the Russian ballet dancer Lydia Lopokova and in 1925, with his former lover, Duncan Grant, as his Best Man, they were married. Keynes was a vociferous advocate of birth control and campaigned against the job discrimination and unequal pay frequently experienced by women. He died in 1946 following a series of exhausting summit meetings in the USA concerning international post-war economic policy. He was 62 years old.

Acknowledgements

This story could not have been told without reference to the many authoritative biographies, commentaries, accounts and research papers on the life and work of the remarkable John Maynard Keynes. These include those written by Robert Skidelsky, Anne Emberton, D.E.Moggridge, Richard Davenport-Hines, David 'Bunny' Garnett, Roy Harrod, J C Wood, Denys Sutton, Trevor Dann, Jason Zweig, Duncan Grant, Tim Harford, Richard Shone, Robert Lekachman, Milo Keynes and of course, Charles Holmes, who was present during some of the extraordinary events described here.

For her excellent paper in *History Today*, Vol. 46, January 1996; Anne Emberton retrieved a number of the letters and notes used here, including those from R.S. Meiklejohn in Chapter 7; from the Keynes and Charleston Papers held by the Modern Archive Centre, King's College Library, Cambridge and from Government documents held by the Public Records Office. Keynes' telegrams to Duncan Grant and Vanessa Bell are from *The Picture Collector*, an essay by Richard Shone and Duncan in *Essays on John Maynard Keynes*, edited by Milo Keynes, published by Cambridge University Press in 1975.

Degas collection research; Ann Dumas, Colta Ives, Susan Alyson Stein, Gary Tinterow et al. Excerpts from William Sharpe's and the Herts war diaries in *1918* by Malcolm Brown and the Imperial War Museum, WW1 accounts: J E Edmonds and A Roberts. Notes on auction techniques: Marina Viatkina.

Special thanks to Tom Davies, archivist at Kings College Cambridge, for affording access to Keynes' original treatise *A Theory of Beauty*.

Wilfred Owen, *Anthem for Doomed Youth*, Winston Churchill, *The World Crisis: 1916-1918*, Siegfried Sassoon, *Aftermath*, Rupert Brooke, *The Soldier*, William Denis Browne & Richard Lovelace, *'To Gratiana Dancing and Singing'*, in various sections including JMK's musings in Chapter 24; John Maynard Keynes, *The Economic Consequences of the Peace* and *The General Theory of Employment, Interest and Money.*

All the paintings used within the main text of the paper edition of this book were sourced through the Imperial War Museum's wonderful collection of WW1 art and are Crown Copyright © IWM. The pieces are:

Victoria Station 1918: The Green Cross Corps (Women's Reserve Ambulance) Guiding Soldiers on Leave. Clare Atwood. IWM ART 2513

Staff Train at Charing Cross Station, London, 1918. Alfred Hayward. IWM ART 1881

The Hotel Christol, Boulogne. Ernest Proctor, 1918. IWM ART 3324

Villa Belle Vue After Air Raid. Adrian Hill, 1918. IWM ART 828

In Sanctuary Wood, Ypres Sector, March 1918. Adrian Hill. IWM ART 541

Dazzle Leave Ships, Boulogne. Charles Bryant, 1917. IWM ART 1346

The watercolour below is by Captain Martin Hardie (1875-1952), war artist and soldier, painted in Boulogne in August 1917. His reports of the conflict, cataloguing the experiences of the troops on the front line as well as a number of his paintings and sketches can be found in *The Hardie Papers* at The Imperial War Museum, Item Number 84/46/1.

Thanks

Immense gratitude for advice and encouragement to my first, gentle readers, Christopher Battiscombe-Scott and Tim Williams, copy editors David Simons and Stephen Harris and to Catherine. Thanks also to Mary Chamberlain, Simon Beaufoy, Rob Warr and David Roberts for wise words and guidance.

At Fitzwilliam College Museum, Cambridge, Emma Darbyshire and colleagues, for their kind facilitation of the use of Cezanne's *Still Life with Apples*.

Toby Eady, Jamie Coleman, Ian Smith, Robert Winder. Anthony Lavers, Deborah Gewirtz, Hannah Gerrish, Miles Keeping, Dan Rapson, Martin Avis, Gina Ennis-Reynolds. Mark Burton, Stephen Yorke.

Morag Joss, James Hawes, Joanne Milne, Ruth Moore, Graham Bird. Marika Leino, Gayle Bell, David Kerekes, Helen Irving, Pascale Lafeber, Sarah-Jane Stretton, Joe Hartshorn, Vicki Churchill & Ella Cunningham.

Katherine, Alexander, Miles and Karen Kearley. William Holborow, Helen Mckendrick. Alexandros van Gilder, Gadi ben Ezer, Bill Ashton, Anthony Heath, Nick French, Susan Harris, Michael Cunningham, Julian Boswell, Philip Roberts, Danielle Valot, David Atwell. Pamela Gyton.

Before turning to creative writing, David Shires was an architect, academic and Reader in Architecture and Design. He is the author of non-fiction textbooks, research papers and journal articles and lives in Oxfordshire.

You can contact David via: davidshiresauthor@gmail.com

Boulogne Harbour near the Louvre Hotel, 1917, by Captain Martin Hardie

Printed in Great Britain
by Amazon

79164103R00162